Mark Coffin of California was barely thirty years old when he won a startling upset victory in his race for a seat in the U.S. Senate. This fact alone would have made him the most talked-about member of that complex and forbidding institution. But Mark was also a bright, handsome, energetic idealist who thought that honesty and decency would be his ticket to political success.

Mark Coffin had a lot to learn—the hard way.

MARK COFFIN, U.S.S. is a magnificent novel of Washington—an insider's view of power at the top, seen through the vivid, fascinating, and totally believable characters created by the master of spellbinding political fiction, Allen Drury.

"Masterful."

Los Angeles Herald-Examiner

"The author of *Advise and Consent* has written another first-rate political novel."

Pittsburgh Press

". . . Drury is absolutely in control of his Washington material in this jet-paced story, and it should prove to be his most popular since *Advise and Consent*. Recommended."

Library Journal

ALLEN DRURY

ace books
A Division of Charter Communications Inc.
A GROSSET & DUNLAP COMPANY
51 Madison Avenue
New York, New York 10010

MARK COFFIN, U.S.S.

An ACE Book, by arrangement with
Doubleday & Company, Inc.

First Ace Printing: June 1980
Published simultaneously in Canada

2 4 6 8 0 9 7 5 3 1
Manufactured in the United States of America

CHARACTERS IN THE NOVEL

In Washington

Mark Coffin, junior senator from California

Linda, his wife

Linnie and Markie, their children

Brad Harper, Mark's administrative assistant

Mary Francesca ("Mary Fran") Garcia, his secretary

Johnny McVickers, his former student and friend

James Rand Elrod, senior senator from North Carolina, Linda's father

Arthur Hampton, senior senator from Nebraska, Majority Leader of the Senate

Herbert Esplin, senior senator from Ohio, Minority Leader

James Monroe Madison, senior senator from California

Janet Hardesty, senior senator from Michigan

Kalakane ("Kal") Tokumatsu, senior senator from Hawaii

Mele, his wife

Clement ("Clem") Chisholm, junior senator from Illinois

Claretta, his wife

Richard ("Rick") Duclos, junior senator from New Hampshire

Pat, his son

Bob Templeton, junior senator from Colorado

Lisette Grayson of ABC

Chuck Dangerfield of "Washington Inside"

Bill Adams of the Associated Press

Lydia ("Lyddie") Bates, a hostess

Chauncey Baron, the Secretary of State

Admiral Sir Harry Fairfield, the British ambassador

Pierre Duchamps DeLatour, the French ambassador

Valerian Bukanin, the Soviet ambassador

Charles Macklin of California ("Good Old Charlie"), a Cabinet nominee

Hamilton ("Ham") Delbacher, the Vice-President

The President

In California
The governor

Harry P. Coffin, publisher of the Sacramento *Statesman,* Mark's father

Margaret, his mother

Dedicated to

The valiant young who, filled with
the disillusions of a decade and
the hope of the ages, still come to
Washington determined to Make It Work

PART
I

1

The machines chatter, the big boards blink, the arrows dart, the markers move. Two anchormen, two anchorwomen, "persons" in another dispensation, peer brightly out of the television screen, chattering away like fury to one another—and to such of the American people as may be listening.

A good many millions are, right now, for this is Election Night.

So-and-So is creeping ahead here.

Such-and-Such is falling behind there.

"You know, it's interesting to see, Mary, how the Blah-Blah faction in the state of Boo-Boo seems to be overcoming the threat posed by the candidacy of Blip-Blip—"

"Yes, Mike, and of course the ethnic vote has undoubtedly had a lot to do with the apparent victory of Blub-Blub in the rural areas of downstate Ho-Ho—"

"To say nothing of the triumph of Baa-Baa in the industrial areas of upstate No-No—"

"Right! And, Peter, as you know, we can't expect that third district to come in for Milkswitch, though the latest returns would seem to indicate that Pooplepot is gaining rapidly in the key city of East Whambledump—"

"Where *naturally,* Eloise, Mayor Squilch is bound to have *some* influence, even if he *has* announced that he will finally retire in 1999—". . .

In other words, the usual stuff—"the customary crap," as they refer to it privately among themselves —while they try to fill in those yawning hours and hold that yawning audience with talk, talk, talk, charts, charts, charts, computers, computers, computers, Importance, Importance, Importance . . .

But suddenly the anchorpersons find something that really intrigues them:

"Let's go to California for a moment, gang! Our man, Joe McGinnis, is out there in Los Angeles right now at the headquarters of the underdog candidate, young Mark Coffin. How does it look in California, Joe?"

A face: young, earnest, pontifical, bearded, shots of City Hall and the Music Center behind.

"Mike, we're beginning to get some smell here of a possible upset—something that could have a direct bearing on both the fate of young Mark Coffin and the fate of the presidential candidate himself, who's beginning to drop very narrowly behind, as you know, all across the country. Now as he comes into the Far West and we begin to get the votes from just-closing California precincts, we're beginning to get just a hint—it's only three precincts so far out of California's more than two thousand, you know, Mike, but some people here seem to think it's significant—that maybe young Mark may pull ahead in this dramatic race between youth and age. And that if he does, he might just conceivably—just possibly, Mike

—pull through the presidential candidate with him. Wouldn't that be something, if the whole presidential election were to be decided by the fate of the youngest senatorial candidate in the country, California's dynamic and attractive young—"

"Thank you, Joe, we have to return to New York now for a minute. Joe's young, too, folks"—a fatherly smile—"and he can't seem to keep his enthusiasm for young Mark Coffin out of his reporting tonight. And I must say it's hard to blame him, when you consider this young man who virtually has come from nowhere to grab the political spotlight in the most populous state in the Union.

"You will remember that just last spring the party nomination seemed sure to go to Charles Macklin, district attorney of Los Angeles County. Opposing him was the most recent ex-governor of California. It appeared the present governor would have to choose between them, thereby possibly compromising his own promising political future. But with a real stroke of political genius he stuck his thumb into the teaching ranks of the political science department at Stanford University and pulled out the plum of young Mark Coffin—so young, in fact, that at the time he was only twenty-nine, and as of this very moment, though he appears on the basis of early returns to be winning the Senate seat, is still a week away from his thirtieth birthday, the constitutional age at which a senator can take office.

"In the months since he won the nomination with the governor's help, he's become perhaps the most appealing, certainly the freshest, face in the whole gallery of national politics. And now if he can pull the presidential candidate in with him—

"Mike, Mike! Joe's on the line again and he says

Mark's now leading 10,253 votes to 9,981, with five precincts reporting. He says they're going crazy out there!"

"Yes, Mary, that really does look like a trend. It's true we still have more than two thousand precincts to go, ladies and gentlemen, but if this trend continues, our computers should soon be predicting a victory for young Mark Coffin. And with him, perhaps, the new President of the United States as well. What a dramatic event that would be! But now let's go to Chicago for a minute and see what's happening out there in that hard-fought Senate race while we await further word of this dramatic upset that seems to be in the making in California—this upset that may well decide not only the California Senate seat but the presidency as well.

"Bob McClendon out there in Chicago, how are things where you are?"

Their voices fade into the background, turned down by a firm and even impatient hand. (Yet, really, why should he be impatient? It's his fate that's being decided, isn't it?) Their ever-so-animated, earnestly smiling, earnestly mouthing faces continue to grimace. Robbed of voices, and with them of Importance, they are abruptly reduced to what they are, little people on a little screen in a living room—a living room casual, comfortable, unpretentious. Through a window in the distance the gleaming floodlit tower of the Hoover library on the Stanford campus accentuates the night. There is an air of excitement, here, too, but it is subdued, cautious, sensible. Nobody here has much faith in computers, long-range predictions, the desperate time-filling burblings of commentators. Everybody here is hopeful but not yet really daring to hope too much: in California the night is still young and there is a long way to go.

Instinctively the occupants of the room—a lithe and beautiful girl of twenty-seven, an earnest college kid of twenty, a pleasant-faced man in his sixties, his equally pleasant-faced wife—turn to the fair-haired, level-eyed, good-looking young man seated before the television set with two sleepy youngsters, Linnie, seven, and Mark, Jr., six, on his lap. Aware that they expect him to say something, be it inane or sensible—just *something,* on this fantastically important night for them all—Mark Coffin of California *(Not even elected yet,* he tells himself wryly, *and already* I'm *calling* me *Mark Coffin of California)* smiles and says,

"Well, I'm glad *they're* optimistic."

"Aren't you?" asks Johnny McVickers, the college kid lounging on the rug beside him.

"Not yet," he says soberly.

"Daddy's going to be President!" Linnie announces, at which they all laugh.

"I believe you, baby," says her mother, Linda, starting to serve the coffee and sandwiches she has just brought from the kitchen. "But one thing at a time."

"Won't it be wonderful if he owes the presidency to you?" Johnny McVickers asks. "He'll be obligated to you for life!"

"I'm not so sure, Johnny," Mark replies soberly, "that I want a man like that to feel he's obligated to me. I doubt if it would make him love me. I'll feel better if he takes California on his own. I'll just think about me and not worry about him, for the time being."

"You're going to make it," Linda says confidently.

"Think so?" he asks, taking her hand and looking up at her.

"I just talked to Daddy in Washington. He's at national headquarters. They're all convinced you've got it sewed up."

"Great," Mark says dryly. "That'll do it for me. Is *he* convinced?"

"Yes, he thinks so. By a very narrow margin—but then, you know Daddy. He always was a conservative."

"I'll bank on Senator Elrod's judgment any time," Mark says.

"Except on a few defense issues," his father remarks with a smile from the sofa across the room.

"And a few foreign policy issues," his mother echoes, beside him.

"That's right," Mark agrees crisply. "On those, we may have some differences. But that's our personal problem."

Actually, of course, it's more than that. In a grand library in Georgetown it's already being discussed by three men who will have much influence on Mark Coffin's senatorial career if he has one. The host is Chauncey Baron, sixty-three, a New Yorker of supreme and icy elegance who has been in and out of the State Department for the past three administrations in one capacity and another. A towering man with a fierce mustache, a frigid gaze and no patience with the fools of this world, of whom he perceives himself to be surrounded by multitudes, he looks the perfect Secretary of State and, in a two-year stint with the previous administration, proved himself to be.

Chauncey is entertaining two of his oldest and dearest friends tonight, Senate Majority Leader Arthur Emmet Hampton of Nebraska and Senate Minority Leader Herbert Esplin of Ohio. Art Hampton is sixty-eight, a spare, dry, decent, patient, compassionate and tolerant man who understands his colleagues' foibles with all the brilliance of a Lyndon Johnson but treats them with all the discreet refusal to take advantage of a Mike Mansfield. Herb Esplin, sixty-five, is a florid orator, a sly wit, an outwardly easygoing, backslapping politician whose amiable aspect disguises one of the most sophisticated political minds of Washington.

The three have known one another for many years, sometimes allies, sometimes opponents, veterans of many a battle on the Hill and in Foggy Bottom.

Muted by Chauncey's hand, as impatient as Mark's, the anchorpersons bubble silently but ever-so-brightly away on the television set that temporarily dominates the room. Chauncey ignores them as he approaches his guests, drinks in hand.

"Is young Mark Coffin going to make it?"

"I just talked to his father-in-law at national headquarters," Art Hampton says. "Jim Elrod says Mark's going to make it by the skin of his teeth."

"And with him," Herb Esplin says, "your distinguished candidate for President."

"Whom you, as Minority Leader of the U.S. Senate," Chauncey says, "just can't wait to welcome to the White House."

"We're going to cut him up in little bits and pieces and spread him all over Pennsylvania Avenue for the crows to eat," Herb Esplin says cheerfully, "and not even my dear friend the distinguished majority leader of the U.S. Senate will be able to put him back together again."

"Well," Art says, "since I'll be leading my gallant little band of seventy-three against your overpowering force of twenty-seven, I think perhaps I'll be able to."

"Ah well," Herb says with airy good humor, "we'll

see. Are you going back to the State Department, Chaunce? Or are you going to remain a private citizen so you can keep on chasing all those Hollywood glamor girls you like so much?"

"Who says I like Hollywood glamor girls?" Chauncey demands blandly. Herb hoots and Art smiles.

"Come on, now, Chaunce," Herb says. "Don't kid your old pals here. Yon stern and dignified austerity hideth a suave pursuer, methinks. That's why we all keep book on you. It's intriguing to see how many young ladies can be successfully seduced by statesmanship, profundity, world-shaking decisions and all that other crap you handle so beautifully."

"Well, at least," Chauncey says, "you admit I *do* handle it beautifully. So who cares what else I handle?"

"Absolutely right," Herb agrees jovially. "So, are you going back to State?"

"If I see this in Jack Anderson's column tomorrow morning," Chauncey Baron says sternly, "I shall shoot you both. But yes, I think I will be nominated —if Mark wins, and if he carries the President in with him."

"How will it feel to be Secretary of State for the second time?" Art inquires.

"Damned depressing, frankly," Chauncey says somberly. "Things are, as usual, in one hell of a mess. Africa is threatening to explode again at any minute, ditto the Middle East, ditto Latin America, ditto Asia, ditto you name it. The Soviets have reached a point in their power build-up where they're about ready to begin some serious bullying and blackmailing, and I'm not sure we have the strength or the will to stand up to them. Other than that, things are in great shape everywhere."

"And yet you and your new President-to-be want to take on the job!" Herb says.

"Somebody has to."

"And you think you can do it best."

"Don't we all think that in Washington, whatever we do?" Art inquires. "We wouldn't be here otherwise."

"What are you going to do with young Mark if he makes it?" Herb asks Art.

"I'd like to see him on the Foreign Relations Committee," Chauncey offers. "Can't you get him on there, Art? He's written a couple of books on America's place in the world that have mightily impressed *me,* even though I don't agree with some of his arguments. I don't know whether you two have read them, but—"

"I haven't," Art says, "but I know he's a smart boy. I don't know how I can get him on that committee, though. We don't have that many seats available. Unless"—his eyes brighten mischievously as he turns to his colleague—"we can persuade the minority to give us a seat."

"Oh no you don't," Herb Esplin says crisply. "But I'll tell you what you can do. You can get old Luther Hanson of Minnesota off there and put Mark in his place."

"Luther would bellow like a wounded moose."

"Nobody likes him, anyway. And I tell you what we'll do in return. We'll bounce Johnny Johnson of New Hampshire, who is in the same category, and replace him with Kal Tokumatsu of Hawaii, whom everybody likes. How's that?"

"God!" Art Hampton exclaims wryly. "All this bloodshed just for a freshman from California."

"I'd appreciate it," Chauncey Baron says quietly. "I could work with him."

"We'll see," Art Hampton says. "I'll have to think about it."

"Do that," Chauncey says, flicking up the volume of the television to find the anchorpersons outdoing themselves. Pennsylvania, North Carolina, Georgia, Vermont, Illinois and Ohio are all toss-ups. Washington and Oregon have definitely gone for the opposition candidate for President. Mark Coffin has increased his lead to 10,000 votes with some one thousand precincts still to be reported. Millimeter by millimeter the presidential candidate, though his margin is less, is creeping up with him. "California may very well be deciding the fate of the nation and the world tonight!" Bubble, bubble, toil and trouble, maps, graphs, lights, computers, talk, talk, talk, smile, smile, smile, strain, strain, strain, Importance, Importance, Importance. Elsewhere in Washington on this cold and blustery night they are also discussing Mark Coffin and his coattail-rider.

In the vast concourse of the Kennedy Center—red carpet, gleaming glass chandeliers, giant two-story windows looking out upon the terrace over the dark Potomac to the deep woods and scattered lights of Virginia—it is intermission. Ten television sets have been established here, too, evenly spaced down the length of the concourse. Crowds are milling about, smoking, laughing, drinking, talking; big groups are gathered around each set. Near one of them the British ambassador, Admiral Sir Harry Fairfield, spare, leathery, bright-eyed, is standing thoughtfully beside stocky, impatient-looking Valerian Bukanin of the Soviet Union and thin, permanently disapproving Pierre Duchamps DeLatour of France.

"Well," Sir Harry says, puffing on a cigarette, "I see our friend may be making it. Thanks to young

Mark Coffin, that is."

"And Britain is pleased," Bukanin observes, not looking very pleased himself.

"The town's become dull lately," Sir Harry says lightly. "I think it will liven things a bit. Might liven 'em for the whole world, in fact."

"The candidate is no friend of France," Pierre DeLatour says dourly.

"Nonsense!" Sir Harry says jovially. "You take your ambassadorial duties too intensely, Pierre. Everyone is a friend to France! As France, of course, is a friend to everyone."

Pierre gives him a sharp look; Bukanin snorts.

"The government of the Soviet Union is not pleased," he says sourly. "More lectures, more moralizing, more meddling! He will be no better than the last one."

"If he has as much cause as the last one," Sir Harry says calmly, "more power to him."

"You are clever," Bukanin says, "but your country is pathetic, so it does not matter."

"Spoken with true Soviet diplomacy," Sir Harry says acidly, while his French colleague looks pleased at his discomfiture.

Bukanin shrugs.

"When one has power, who needs diplomacy?"

"Not as much power as you think, I venture," Sir Harry says, "when *that* one"—gesturing to the television set on which a single face is momentarily appearing—"becomes President."

"He is not President yet," Bukanin says.

"And if he becomes so," Pierre DeLatour remarks, "he will owe it to this young Mark Coffin, will he not? Therefore I shall spend some time cultivating young Mark Coffin."

"So will we all, I dare say," Sir Harry agrees. "I

believe in cultivating all the new ones, particularly in the Senate. It has great influence on American foreign policy."

"Ha!" Bukanin snorts. "It takes no great intelligence to support a policy of bullying and meddling!"

"True," Sir Harry murmurs, bland once more, and again Valerian looks at him sharply. "Alas, how true."

"Well," Pierre says as bells begin to ring and the crowd begins to drift back into the three theaters of Kennedy Center, "we shall see what these young ones have to offer. Mark Coffin may be the most important of all, but there are others."

"Yes," Sir Harry agrees. "It promises to be an interesting 'freshman class,' as they call it. Good night, Valerian. Her Majesty's Government hope the government of the Soviet Union will not be too overwhelmed by today's results."

"Ha!" Bukanin says, gives him a look, turns on his heel and stalks off.

"Do you hope young Mark Coffin and his candidate win?" Pierre inquires as they watch him plod away, and then begin to walk through the throng toward their waiting wives.

"Devoutly," Sir Harry says.

"So do we," the French ambassador agrees. "And along with many other stout hearts as well."

The crowd thins, the concourse gradually becomes almost deserted, but Mike the anchorperson is still hard at work.

"And up there in Vermont we've got an interesting Senate race, too, though it isn't having the national impact of the race in California because the presidential candidate has already carried the state. In this instance *he* appears to be carrying the candidate for the Senate—Lieutenant Governor Richard 'Rick' Duclos—that's spelled D-u-c-l-o-s but pronounced *Du-cloh,* ladies and gentlemen—an attractive young liberal who comes to the national scene with a reputation for good government and an equally notable reputation as a political Romeo. Washington has already seen a good deal of Rick Duclos in recent months, when he's been down there on frequent visits as his state's emissary seeking federal funds. We understand he's already fluttered a good many feminine hearts in the capital, and now as a United States Senator he's bound to flutter even more. Let's go to Vermont and see what's happening to Rick Duclos—"

But although the camera eye is in Duclos headquarters in Montpelier, a scene of much excitement with large banners and posters of the candidate, he is nowhere to be found.

"Well," Mike says as campaign aides can be seen running about, wildly agitated, trying to find their candidate to take advantage of this national exposure, "at the moment Rick doesn't seem to be available, so we'll take you back to California now to see what's new with young Mark Coffin—"

His voice trails away, the agitated campaign staffers fade from the nation's sight. In a far back room of the hotel that houses his headquarters the candidate, unaware of the search for him because he has a more pressing matter on his hands, is backed up against the door, pinned by a very upset young lady.

"You aren't going to do this to me, Rick Duclos!" she cries angrily as she struggles into her dress, he into his trousers. "I've kept quiet all through this campaign when I could have blown it sky-high. God, *why didn't I?* Why was I ever so stupid as to let you persuade me that you really wanted to marry me?

'You'll be Mrs. Senator Rick Duclos.' Oh hell, yes! What a stupid fool I've been!"

"No, you haven't," Rick says, turning on the charm as much as possible in the midst of his hasty struggle to resume his clothes. "You've been everything to me."

" 'Everything to you!' Don't give *me* that corny crap! Unless you announce our marriage tonight I'm going to tell the whole wide world what a cheat you are. I'm going to tell everybody! *I'm going on television!* I'll *destroy* you!" And, by now half-presentable, she tries to dodge around him.

"You can't do that!" he exclaims in genuine alarm, gripping the door and refusing to budge. "Now, you listen to me. I told you that I was going to take you to Washington—"

"As Mrs. Senator Rick Duclos!"

"As Mrs. Senator Rick Duclos. And what makes you think I didn't mean it? As soon as I get settled—"

"Ha!"

"As soon as I get settled, I'll send for you and you'll be down there in a jiffy—"

"You bet I will!"

"—in a jiffy, and then we'll get it all arranged. So what's the problem?"

"But why can't you announce it tonight?" she asks, beginning to sound somewhat mollified.

"Strategy," he says solemnly, and she begins to flare up again. But he talks fast and she calms down. "It isn't that I don't love you, and it isn't that I don't have big plans for you—"

"To be Mrs. Senator Rick Duclos."

"To be Mrs. Senator Rick Duclos," he echoes, gritting his teeth. "But there's timing in these matters. You can't just barge into something in politics, you have to have *timing*. Now, when I get down there, you just sit tight—"

"In your law office in Montpelier. I'll be there. Where in hell else would I go?"

"—and when it's right, I'll send for you, and there'll be a big announcement and everything will be O.K."

"Really?" she asks uncertainly.

"Really," he assures her with great sincerity.

"Well—"

"And now, luv"—briskly—"I really must get back out there. I think the tide's turning and I'm beginning to win, and I've got to be on hand for the media. So why don't you slip out first and I'll be along in a couple of minutes?"

"Oh, Rick," she says, dissolving suddenly as he draws her tenderly toward him and prepares a positively magnificent kiss.

"Trust me, baby," he says passionately. *"Trust me."*

There is a knock on the door, a young voice, abrupt, embarrassed.

"Dad! They want you out there!"

"O.K.," Rick calls, coming up for air. "Run along now, honey." He opens the door and pushes her out, giving his tie a last tug as he does so. She goes, exchanging a sharply hostile glance with the dark gangling kid of eighteen who stands in the hall.

"Thanks, Pat," Rick says with hearty relief as they watch the girl disappear. "You saved me just in time."

He starts to put his arm around his son but Pat isn't having any. He shrugs it off roughly and stalks down the hall ahead of his father.

"Well, O.K.," Rick says with a jauntiness that doesn't quite come off. "Well, O.K., if that's the way you feel."

Down the hall there is a burst of shouts and lights as he straightens himself defiantly and goes to meet his triumph. But his eyes are bleak and unhappy for a moment before he puts on his smile and the crowd swallows him up.

At the same moment on Washington's fashionable Foxhall Road, haunt of former Vice-Presidents and others financially able to achieve the neighborhood, the guests at a formal black-tie dinner party in a beautiful white-porticoed house are now strewn about the enormous living room on chairs, sofas, ottomans, the floor—glasses in hand, eyes and ears attentive to the latest from Mike the anchorperson, still gallantly plugging along as the hour nears 1 A.M. in the East, 10 P.M. on the West Coast.

"—in Colorado, where the suddenly tragic figure of young Bob Templeton, thirty-six, has won overwhelming election to the Senate. It was just a week ago, as you all remember, that Senator-elect Templeton's wife and two daughters were killed in the crash of the family plane when they were on their way to join him for a campaign rally. Prior to this tragic event, his election had been considered a certainty, but today's results seem to indicate that he has, understandably, received an enormous sympathy vote as well. Robert Templeton, new United States Senator from Colorado, a man who takes to Washington a ravaged heart but great promise as a legislator, is expected to—"

"Tell me," a woman's voice inquires, "is this your first Election Night party at Lyddie's?"

"You know it is, darling," rejoins another. "How long have you been coming, since 1916?"

"Not quite, sweetie, but long enough to have left the category of gate-crasher and be considered a Real Friend."

"Well!"

The arch conversation, whatever its potentials, is terminated by the entry of Lydia Bates, drenched in diamonds, rubies, emeralds and pearls; at eighty-three Washington's acknowledged hostess with the mostest, who knows everyone, invites everyone, tosses everyone together in parties that sometimes erupt into major arguments and news stories. Lyddie is the widow of the late Speaker of the House Tillman Bates of Illinois, who is so late—some twenty-one years, by now—that Lyddie has long since become a Washington institution in her own right. Possessed of enormous wealth left her by her father—"Daddy was something big and mysterious in the anthracite industry"—she has used it to fund and support, unknown to the public, many charitable causes at home and abroad. But she has reserved a few millions of it—"my fun money," she calls it—for the sole purpose of entertaining and being part of the Washington that so thoroughly entertains her. An invitation to "Lyddie's on Foxhall Road" is a command invitation. Her house, "Roedean," is the only private home to which all Presidents irrespective of party will go. She is one of those perennially chipper, eternally bright, eternally mischievous and delightful old ladies who ought to be allowed to live to 110 because they enjoy life so. Still a beauty and charmer at eighty-three, she is bright as a button, sharp as a razor and generous as the Potomac is wide. She wouldn't live anywhere else, do anything other than what she does. She and Washington are perfectly met. Many a promising young career has been socially launched under Lyddie's wing; and now she thinks she sees another one coming.

"Now, listen, everybody," she cries, clapping her hands. "We're going to make bets. We're all agreed California is the key to it, right?"

"Right!"

"All right, then, we want to know, first, the time when the decision will be final—"

"My God, Lyddie, that may be six A.M.!"

"You're all perfectly welcome, I have twenty beds and the rest of you can sleep on the floor—and we want to know who's going to win the presidency and we want to know if Mark Coffin is going to be senator. And we want to know your best guess as to the margin of each one's victory. So, Jan darling, if you will assist in passing out these pencils and sheets of paper—"

"Can we trust a United States Senator, even one from Michigan?" somebody calls, and laughter greets the tall, gray-haired woman who comes forward to Lyddie's side: Senator Janet Hanson Hardesty, at sixty still strikingly handsome, always beautifully dressed, beautifully coifed, beautifully organized; a dynamo of high intelligence and great intuition, possessed of a steel-trap mind that is usually a match for any of her male colleagues in the Senate and sometimes more than a match for all of them put together. Tonight she is wearing one of her characteristically simple, characteristically expensive dresses, something floating, in a misty rose pink, with her trademark diamond brooch in the shape of a spray of flowers pinned to her left shoulder.

"Let's make it bipartisan, then," Jan Hardesty suggests with a smile. "Clem Chisholm, come up here!"

Across the room obediently rises another of those who will have much to do with Mark Coffin's senatorial career if he has one: a solidly built good-looking gentleman of forty, Illinois's first black senator, Clement Chisholm, former mayor of Springfield, a political sensation when he defied the machine and won an upset victory two years ago. His wife Claretta, an ex-model and still a beauty at thirty-nine, pushes him forward with a shove as everyone laughs and applauds.

When the two senators, both tall, handsome and striking, flank Lyddie with great distinction, she looks up at them with her bright birdlike glance.

"Now, then, dears," she says. "Jan, you take half of these slips of paper, which will be—Lord, how many of you *did* I invite to this party? Was it sixty? No, that was four years ago. Forty-six, that's it. Jan, you count out twenty-three and give the rest to Clem—"

"Suppose she only gives me twenty-two?" Clem inquires with a smile.

"Now," Jan says with mock severity, "the minority would never give the majority a fast count, you know that, Clem. Lyddie will make sure we're both honest."

"That's right, dear," Lyddie says, beaming, as Jan counts to twenty-three in a firm voice and hands the remainder to Clem, who chuckles and of course doesn't bother to count as they start to distribute the tallies among the guests.

"I do hope this new President will be all right," Lyddie says thoughtfully as she watches them. "And I hope this young Mark Coffin will be a nice boy, too. We do so need some nice people in Washington."

"Lyddie, dear, that isn't very flattering," somebody calls. "What about us?"

"Oh, I know, but you're *old* nice people. I want some *new* nice people."

"You mean people you can mold, Lyddie—people you can *twist* and *turn* to your own devious purposes—"

"I just mean people I'd like to entertain," Lyddie says cheerfully. "But then"—looking about—"I guess my standards aren't really all *that* high, are they?"

"Oh, Lyddie, you're impossible!"

"You're outrageous!"

"You're—" and so on, until someone calls sharply, "Quiet, everybody! There's something new coming in on California!"

And as they cluster forward around the television set, it appears that California is indeed heating up. Mark's lead is beginning to climb a little, from 10,000 votes to about 20,000, with some three hundred precincts still to be counted. The presidential candidate's margin, though less than Mark's, is climbing in tandem, precinct by precinct.

It is obvious that Mark is indeed carrying the President with him.

They find, with a quick switch of channels, that one of the networks has already conceded the state to both Mark and the President. The other two, including the by now rather haggard quartet with whom the evening began, are not quite yet ready to do so. It is obvious, however, that their tension is mounting, as it is at Lyddie's on Foxhall Road; and as it is at national headquarters on Connecticut Avenue.

A big, bare, brightly lighted room filled with posters, tables, desks, typewriters, new ticker tape, confetti waiting to be thrown. The usual mix of old pros and young enthusiasts clad in everything from black tie to blue jeans. The sort of great excited hodgepodge that is a headquarters on Election Night.

Three are standing aloof on the edge of the hubbub, watching it with a shrewd professional gaze: a stocky, white-haired man of sixty; an obviously brisk and superior young gentleman of twenty-eight; and a pretty and obviously knowledgeable girl of twenty-six. Their badges, headed MEDIA, identify them: BILL ADAMS, ASSOCIATED PRESS; CHUCK DANGERFIELD, "WASHINGTON INSIDE"; LISETTE GRAYSON, ABC.

"You're the man with the experience, Bill," Chuck begins, and then shouts over the clamor as Bill cups a hand in mock deafness. "I SAID YOU'RE THE MAN

WITH THE EXPERIENCE. Tell us what's going to happen."

"I think we've got a brand-new President and a brand-new baby United States Senator. Don't you kids think so?"

"I'd like to, on both counts," Lisette says, "but I'm learning to be cautious in my old age. We still have three hundred precincts to go."

"A mere bagatelle," Chuck says airily. "God, will it be great to see a new face in the White House!"

"*And* in the Senate," Bill says.

"Even if he is still wearing his Pampers, as the L.A. *Times* put it the other day," Lisette says with a laugh.

"Have you met him?" Chuck asks. "He's really quite a guy. He's a hell of a nice fellow, actually. And he has a delightful wife, too."

"Is he a liberal?" Lisette inquires.

"He's *sexy,*" Chuck assures her solemnly. "What more do you want?"

"I want to know if he's liberal," Lisette says, a trifle impatiently.

"He's a nice guy," Chuck repeats. "I think I can agree with him on a lot of things. I think you can, too."

"Good," Lisette says. "Now, about his being sexy—"

"Honey," Bill Adams says, "I think the first thing I'm going to say to him is, 'Watch out for our Lisette. She's dynamite.' "

"He's a big boy," Lisette says cheerfully. "I dare say he can take care of himself."

"I dare say Linda will take care of him, too," Chuck remarks. "She's not Senator Elrod's daughter for nothing. Plus which, she's a damned attractive gal herself. I wouldn't try to move in, if I were you."

"You're obviously planning to move in, as a friend," Lisette observes. "I'll move in, too—as a friend. Anyway, I think he's going to be a damned good news source, so I'll cultivate him."

"He isn't in yet," Bill points out, but just then there's a wild, ecstatic whoop and the room explodes in sound.

"Oh yes he is!" Chuck shouts. "And so's the President!"

Confetti flies, voices babble, faces and bodies whirl in a wild fandango of celebration. A new day has dawned, and at national headquarters a thousand hopefuls are ecstatically preparing to climb on board.

At the modest home on the Stanford campus everyone is wildly happy, too. Mark's living room is crowded with excited friends and supporters. Linda is in his arms, crying. Linnie and Mark, Jr., are standing beside them bewildered but happy. Mark's parents, hand in hand, are dancing a jig. The telephone is ringing insistently and outside there is the growing murmur of many people.

Presently Mark disengages himself gently from Linda with a final jubilant kiss and reaches for the phone. Abruptly his expression sobers, his voice becomes respectful. The room falls swiftly silent.

"Yes, it is, Mr. President," he says, "a great victory . . . Well, congratulations to you, too, sir, I couldn't be more delighted . . . Oh, thank you, but you could have done it without me. I couldn't have done it without you."

"*Mark Coffin!*" Linda hisses. "You could, *too!* Don't you tell him that! He got in on your coattails, and don't you let him forget it!"

"Thank you, Mr. President," Mark says, smiling and waving her away. "Yes, I look forward very much to working with you, too. I think it's going to be a great administration, a great challenge. Yes, sir . . . Well, you know you can always count on me."

"He *cannot!*" Linda hisses again, all her instincts as a senatorial daughter and child of politics aroused. "Don't let him think that!"

"Yes, sir," Mark says. "Yes, thank you. I'll see you in Washington. Yes, sir. Good night . . . Well"—turning back—"that was nice of him."

"Nice of him, nothing!" Linda snorts. "He knows he owes his victory to you, and don't you ever humble yourself to him, Mark Coffin!"

"Well," Mark says, "he *is* going to be the President."

"But *you're* going to be Senator Mark Coffin," Linda says fiercely. "And that's only the beginning!"

"Maybe," he replies with an affectionate smile. "Maybe."

"No maybes," Linda says firmly. "Nothing but yeses, from here on in."

"Mark!" his father calls from across the room. "Some special people here to see you."

Mark and Linda step forward to the door, his arm around her. They are greeted with a roar of welcome by what must be at least a thousand jubilant Stanford students massed on the lawn and filling the street. Somebody leads them in a cheer: "Give 'em the ax, the ax, the ax!" Somebody else begins to sing the Stanford Hymn. Instantly it is taken up by a thousand voices.

Linda starts crying again, and Mark's eyes also fill with tears as they stand and wave while the singing mounts. But behind Mark's tears a somber expression grows in his level gray eyes.

Suddenly the fun and games are over.

Suddenly it is all real.

Ahead lies the United States Senate and a world, seemingly in permanent disarray, for which he is now, in some substantial measure, responsible.

2

Two hours later, the kids bedded down, his parents safely tucked away in the guest room, the media, the friends, the students and well-wishers all dispersed and the neighborhood at last returned to quiet, he lay awake for perhaps another hour after he and Linda had completed their wild, exultant coupling. She lay curled beside him exhausted and, for the moment at least, at peace, her soft, rhythmical breathing as much a part of him after eight years of marriage as his own deeper and more troubled respirations. He wished he could achieve the same abandonment to sleep, but he could not. Perhaps, he thought bleakly, he never could again.

"Young Mark Coffin," as he was apparently destined to be known nationally for quite some time to come, was not resting easy on this night of his sensational and unexpected triumph.

Not that it had been quite as unexpected for him as it had been for everyone else—with the possible exception, he acknowledged, of Linda and his parents. He had felt for some weeks now that he would win; a conviction he could not quite justify, for reasons he could not quite define, but very strong within him nonetheless. He had told himself on numerous occasions that it was just ego, he was just a cocky kid who thought he could lick the whole wide world, just plain-dumb flat-out arrogant—and yet he could not shake the sense of his own destiny which had carried him through all the rare adversities and rather consistent triumphs of a short and favored life.

Short and *overly* favored, he thought now as he reviewed its major passages in the light of the great demands that were about to be made upon him; short, overly favored and perhaps not altogether preparatory for the life he was about to embark upon. He was student enough of history, observer enough of his senatorial father-in-law, Jim Elrod, perceptive enough in his own heart and being, so that he had at least some conception of the task he faced. Hundreds of millions of people, he told himself ironically, were thinking of him tonight as the brightest, luckiest, most exciting and most enviable young figure on the national scene. He had enjoyed that feeling for perhaps half an hour after his victory became final. Then it had seeped away, probably, he recognized glumly, never to return.

Because what was he, after all? An attractive, intelligent, well-meaning, idealistic, easygoing—kid. He had never felt older and more capable, or, simultaneously, younger and more incompetent. You're a fluke, Mark Coffin, he told himself with something close to bitterness; a media-created, politically accidental, fantastically lucky fluke. And what makes you think you are worthy of what the whole world now expects of you?

Looking back at his sensational—or at least sensationally climaxed—career, he could see now that it had been adequate but not really distinguished by any of the standards he was suddenly setting for himself. Adequate enough by yesterday's standards, maybe, but not by tonight's, tomorrow's, and all the tomorrows after that. Mark Eldridge Coffin, junior United States Senator from the State of California . . . well, *get you!*

To begin with, he could not even claim that he had worked his way up from the modest background so beloved of political mythologizers. Not every red-blooded American boy had a father who was editor and publisher of the Sacramento *Statesman,* that prosperous daily that had influenced California politics for more than a hundred years and under Harry P. Coffin's astute if somewhat conservative tutelage had continued to do so all the days of Mark's life. Not every red-blooded American boy had heard from childhood that he would probably some day achieve a political career and most certainly would achieve a major publication with which to influence his times. Not every red-blooded American boy had been given the feeling from his earliest youth that he was born into what his quiet mother once candidly—and controversially—referred to as "the group that really runs things." A lot of red-blooded American boys had rebelled against things like this, thereby causing themselves, their parents and all about them a lot of unnecessary anguish while achieving very little with their rebellion. Not Mark Coffin. Mark Coffin had always been a good boy.

Too good, he supposed: very little had disturbed the easy upward progressions of his life. No particular rebellions or awkwardnesses had occurred. He had been blessed with good looks, an intelligent and inquisitive mind, a likable personality, a happy nature. The small bumps of childhood had come and gone without affecting any of them. A consistently good scholar, yet modest and self-deprecating enough so that he escaped the customary resentments of schoolmates less fortunate and more lazy, he managed to be popular with his teachers without being labeled teacher's pet. And when he moved on to Stanford he managed to pass through the campus turmoil of the late sixties with the unbroken liking and respect of his peers, whatever their political persuasions. He was just too solid, too steady, too self-contained and too friendly for resentments to gather around him. Again, he felt now in the lonely reaction from his triumph, it had probably all been too goody-good.

And yet he couldn't honestly be other than he was. Now and again there had been those who tried to challenge this, seeking to push him this way or that politically, this way or that scholastically, this way or that sexually. He had learned an inner reserve from such episodes that he had not had before: that much had changed. To every attempt to invade what he presently came to refer to in his own mind as "my castle," he returned a smiling, unruffled, and unoffended response that did not satisfy but did manage to placate. He remembered reflecting wryly when he graduated that he had probably left behind him more unsatisfied would-be manipulators of his being—who at the same time remained genuine friends—than anyone who had passed through the Stanford Farm in quite some time.

Not the least of these were the various girls who thought Mark Coffin would be the best possible catch anyone could have. Several breached the castle enough to get inside it physically, and, in one case, emotionally as well; but none quite achieved the necessary impact to win the complete conquest she sought. He was heart-whole and reasonably fancy-free when he went to Washington to spend the summer after graduation "keeping an eye on the California delegation," as his father put it, in the *Statesman's* three-man bureau. Linda Rand Elrod changed all that two weeks after he arrived.

He could remember now as vividly as the day it happened his first glimpse of the complex of emotions, impulses, idealisms, ambitions, kindnesses and irritations with which he had just engaged in nature's most intimate activity. He knew her little better now, he suspected, than he did then; the essential core remained as hidden from him as his probably did from her. In this he knew they were no different from most married couples on the face of the earth, and he supposed his lingering regret about it was no different from anyone else's; certainly, he was sure, no different from hers. Yet they had "a very good marriage," as it was known, and in truth he knew very well that this was exactly what it was.

He had been hanging around the bureau—where he was supposed to put in a few months to "get a taste of Washington" before starting the teaching career that he and his parents knew would probably be only a temporary detour before he returned to Sacramento and the executive offices of the paper—when he had been assigned one day to cover a subcommittee meeting of the Senate Foreign Relations Committee. It was his first visit to the Capitol and that, too, fixed the day forever in his mind. Driving down Pennsylvania Avenue toward the great building gleaming ahead on the Hill, white and pristine-looking against the humid summer sky, he felt an excitement, perhaps even a premonition (though that might be retrospective now) as the cab sped up the curving drive and deposited him beneath the archway on the stone steps he would come to know very well then, and now would know so much better.

He had found his way upstairs to the Press Gallery, received directions from the helpful staff, found his way downstairs again to the subcommittee room hidden away among the arches painted by Brumidi; found himself a seat at the press table, shyly at first but more easily when he was welcomed with friendly smiles; found himself staring with great interest at his first United States Senator, James Rand Elrod of North Carolina; found himself a second later staring with even greater interest at the beautiful young girl who sat in a chair just behind the senator, leaning forward from time to time to offer papers, memos, a whispered word.

He judged her to be a couple of years younger than himself, which turned out to be correct, and sensed immediately that she was already a veteran of this exciting new world of Washington. He was too new and too shy to ask questions, but presently one of his elders leaned over with a smile and whispered, "That young lady you're so taken with is Linda Rand Elrod, the senator's daughter." He started and blushed, unaware he had been so obvious. Just at that moment she looked up, caught his eye, and after a second's appraisal, gave him a sudden dazzling smile before she turned quickly back to scanning the papers in her hand. Across the table his informant chuckled in a kindly way, and he blushed some more. But when she glanced up again he was ready for it. Smile answered smile, and he knew with a sudden profound conviction that he was going to see much, much more of Linda Rand Elrod.

Before the summer was out they were dating steadily, Jim Elrod had tacitly given them his blessing, and she had already decided she would come out to Stanford for her senior year. This had upset the senator at first—"Linda Rand's been my right hand ever since her mother died, and I'm not so sure I want to let her go 'way out West with you wild and woolly Yankees, young man"—but presently, realizing that he had finally met a force somewhat greater than he was in her young life, he conceded with a gracefully humorous smile and a prediction that none of them believed at the time.

"Well, I expect it'll only be temporary. If she does marry you, Mark"—nobody had mentioned this so far, and once again he was startled, and blushed—"I'm not saying she will, now, but if she does, I wouldn't be a bit surprised to see her comin' back here some day as both the daughter and the wife of a United States Senator. I really wouldn't, now."

"Oh, I don't think so, Senator," he said, and meant it. "But if it ever happened," he added with a sudden smile, "I couldn't want a better model than you to pattern myself after."

Which of course did him no harm with Jim Elrod, who by now was obviously as convinced as Linda that nothing could be more felicitous. So, after her last year as a student and his first as a teaching assistant in the political science department, they were married and lived—happily?—ever after.

Yes, he would have to say happily, as they lay side by side eight years later, parents of two, newly minted golden figures of the national pantheon, suddenly tonight the most famous young pair in the country—proof that Jim Elrod's prediction had been as exact as many of his other shrewd judgments of men and events. Yet surely it must have been sheer happenstance that made him pull that remark out of the blue; that or an instinctive understanding of Mark—and an absolute knowledge of his daughter.

Linda, child of politics, had announced at fifteen that she was going to marry a senator like Daddy. Jim Elrod, then forty-eight and four years into his first term, had greeted this with a laugh that started to be a little patronizing but changed hastily to one of respect when he saw her absolutely earnest and solemn expression.

"You're sure you really want that, baby?" he asked, tousling the hair that was still today as full and golden as it had been then. "It's a tough life, being a senator's wife." "Mommy did it," she said—the first time, he realized, that she had used the endearment since the skidding auto accident on a dark swamp road three years before that had abruptly removed the brightest thing in both their lives. "Well," he had said, his mind and heart flooding with many things—sadness, regret, desolation, guilt—many things, "I guess she would like you to do it, too, if you want to. But don't fool yourself: it isn't easy being a senator's wife." "I know," she said in a tone that made him realize suddenly that she had probably known more than he ever suspected, "but I'm tough."

And so she was, his "right hand" who had been his only child and, after her mother's death, his principal companion. At seventeen she became his official hostess, beginning the series of small monthly dinners that soon were to become famous on the Hill. The same year he brought her into the office during her summers home from Smith; and a year later when she met Mark Coffin, she really was his right hand, not always agreeing with his conservative view of things, but always there as sounding board, idea-challenger, confidante, companion, adviser—understander.

Foolishly, he knew, he would dream from time to time that this situation might continue unchanged, but he knew he had a very bright, very determined and very beautiful daughter, and he was not really surprised when nature took its course. He was a little surprised, at first, that it had happened so early; but as he came to know Mark, he began to think that perhaps Linda had chosen more shrewdly than she knew. Their potentials together were very great.

Mark was handsome as she was beautiful. There was about him at twenty-two an air of steadiness and maturity considerably beyond his years, plus the easygoing generosity and good will that drew most people instinctively to him. And he was heir to the Sacramento *Statesman,* even though he appeared to be engaged in some sort of mild rebellion against the family destiny that was taking him out of the newspaper business into the academic life. When Senator Elrod met Harry and Margaret Coffin he knew that they regarded this as a temporary aberration that would presently yield to what Margaret in her gently firm way called "the realities."

At first Jim Elrod thought this, too; but the more he studied his son-in-law, the more he decided Mark knew what he was doing. The *Statesman* was a generally conservative paper: Mark would separate himself from this by joining the teaching staff at Stanford, where he would be free to express his own ideas and not be tied to his father's. At the same time he would get out from under the burden of the paper's reputation among California voters whose often erratic swings between conservatism and liberalism did so much to give the state's politics their reputation for crazy-quilt unpredictability. And he would write a book or two, which he proceeded to do, which would distinguish him even further as his own man. Mark, Jim Elrod decided quite early, knew exactly what he was doing; though he did not quite see how Mark would make it from the Stanford campus to the national arena.

And actually, Mark thought now, he had wondered sometimes himself. He remembered the number of times his father-in-law had said, "You ought to be in the Senate, boy, but I'm blamed if I see how you're goin' to get there from Palo Alto. You've got to get into the mainstream. Can't swim with the big fish off there in a little puddle on the side."

"Stanford," he always objected mildly, "isn't a little puddle, Jim. And anyway, maybe I don't want to be in the Senate."

"Maybe I don't want to be in the White House," Senator Elrod replied humorously, "but like all senators over thirty and under ninety, I'd rather like to have the chance."

So would he, Mark acknowledged silently, so would he. And here he was on the first rung of the ladder, so apparently his strategy had paid off after all.

Not that it was at first a conscious strategy, and not that he had ever really acknowledged to Linda that he had one; but bit by bit, sometimes not very clearly or directly but always with a general drift, he seemed to have been able to shape things that way. On many occasions Linda had suggested that he run for office locally, "just to get your feet wet." Each time he had gently repulsed the idea, until finally one day, in a rare show of exasperation, she had snapped, "Well, I guess you're always just going to be a stick-in-the-mud professor, then!"

"Getting to be a better-known one," he pointed out—again, mildly, because she had great ambitions for him and her devotion to him and his welfare was absolute. "I've written a book that hasn't been so badly received, I'm working on another, I'm getting along well here. Why," he said with a teasing glance, "I may be dean of the poli sci department some day. Who could ask for anything more?"

"Oh, Mark, for heaven's sake!" she said, still impatient but beginning to smile at his teasing. "You're not going to be content with that, and you know it."

"Certainly you're not, anyway," he observed, and she nodded with a sudden thoughtful frown.

"That's right. Washington is in my blood, and I want it. I want it for me, but more than that I want it for you. You've got the ability, Mark. When I think of all the jackasses I've seen on that Hill—"

"You think one more wouldn't hurt the country," he completed with a chuckle. "Well, maybe not. But it's a long way from Stanford to the Hill, as your dad points out to me from time to time."

"Not if you play your cards right," she said. "You can always work it through the governor."

"I'm aware of the governor," he agreed, "as indeed, who is not? I'm working on him."

"Mark Coffin," she said, dropping into his lap for a sudden kiss, "I'll bet you have it all figured out already."

"I'm working on it," he said, returning the kiss with interest. "A little more yogurt, and I'll have it made."

But there was of course more to California's governor than the yogurt-eating, self-conscious, humble-pie down-to-earthiness that made him such an easy target for the sarcasms of the press. (The voters loved it, so who cared what a few columnists and editorial writers had to say about it?) For one thing, he had been encouraged in his career, and really been boosted into statewide prominence, by Harry Coffin, a lifelong friend of his father's. The Sacramento

Statesman was the first paper in California to hail the youthful mayor of Pasadena as an up-and-coming potential for the governor's mansion. (One thing he did do after he got in was live there, unlike one predecessor who had made a well-publicized point of non-occupation.) Once the ball had begun rolling it had picked up a surprising momentum: California's electorate was once again itchy and anxious for a change. A "walk-the-state" campaign and a carefully calculated television blitz (financed principally by the oil companies, upon whom he turned with noble fanfare immediately after election, which did not surprise them and made him great points with a lot of people) brought him into office at thirty-four. With great skill he managed to please enough of the people enough of the time so that the many who viewed him with considerable skepticism were successfully fooled and frustrated. Even Harry P. Coffin, who thought he had backed a conservative, still thought so, although he was forced to admit from time to time that "some things" made him "a little uneasy." They were always carefully balanced by "some things" on the other side. The governor, bland, equivocal, and as difficult to attack as a fog bank over his native San Francisco, sailed along happily. So far Harry Coffin had not asked any particular favors in return for his early support; but Mark was sure he would if his son requested it.

Furthermore, his own relationship with the governor was close, since the governor had become a family intimate when Harry Coffin adopted him politically, and the closeness in age between Mark and himself had soon made them good friends. He told Mark frequently that he considered Mark "the first man in my brain trust," and made a great point of consulting him about many things. Mark noted, however, that he never really took his advice on anything, and also that he kept their relationship an informal one, with no offers of a job in Sacramento. Mark probably would not have accepted in any event, being by then well ensconced at Stanford; and he presently came to feel that it was just as well to be referred to in the media as "a member of the governor's shadow cabinet." It gave him the aura without the responsibility, an air of mysterious influence that glamorized him for his students and could not help but impress his teaching colleagues, even though the more jealous faculty gossips tried to denigrate his influence and play down his standing in Sacramento. He knew it didn't mean much himself, but he wasn't about to tell them that; and it was only when California's senior United States senator died after a long illness that he suddenly perceived that things might at last fall into place for the ambitions he was beginning to nurture. Even so, the governor's decision came as a surprise. It was logical, from the governor's standpoint, but still surprising.

Two candidates, divided as usual between northern and southern California, loomed for the party's nomination in the coming national election that would take into office both a new senator from California and a President of the United States. One, an aging former governor of the state, came from Eureka on the far northern coast; the other, Charles Macklin, was the stoutly law-and-order district attorney of Los Angeles County. The former governor was the darling of the state's liberals; Charlie Macklin led the troops of Orange County and the state's equally vociferous conservatives. The governor was caught neatly in the middle between the two contending wings of his party. His chagrin was concealed but inescapable, since he planned to run for re-election two years hence and then make a bid for the presidential nomination two years after that. It was no time to take sides with one faction or the other. Something had to be done, particularly since Harry Coffin, the governor's own first booster, had been a friend since childhood of Charlie Macklin and had, more times than once, murmured to his family that if he'd had any sense he would have helped send Charlie to Sacramento instead of the two-faced puzzle he *had* supported.

When intimations of this mood began to appear in strong editorials in the *Statesman* backing Macklin for the senatorial nomination, echoed by a good many other papers up and down the state, the governor told his press conference amiably that he would "have to put on my thinking cap" and make a decision.

"Please do," the dean of Capitol correspondents requested dryly, "since the primary is little more than three weeks away."

"Just the right time to decide, isn't it?" the governor inquired with a happy smile; and about eleven o'clock that night had done so with a couple of quick telephone calls.

"Harry," he said in the first one, "I've decided we've got to break the deadlock between Macklin and Governor Davis by getting a new face into the race."

"Who?" Harry Coffin asked skeptically. "You?"

"No, sir," the governor said crisply. "Mark Coffin, whom I believe you know."

For several seconds there was no response. Then Harry P. Coffin said, "Well, I'll be damned!" Then he said, "You clever bastard!" And then he said,

"Whoooooeeeee! Margaret! Come here and see if you hear what I hear from this screwy, marvelous character!"

That took care of Harry P. Coffin, who was back in the fold with a vengeance. It left the call to Mark.

"Hi," the governor said two minutes later. "Everybody watching the news?"

"Yes, we are, Larry," Linda said, her voice getting the slight defensive edge it acquired with him. "What can we do for you?"

"You can help me make tomorrow morning's news something worth listening to. Is your able and distinguished husband there?"

"Yes," she said cautiously, and he could almost hear her trained Washington mind reacting to these rhetorical adjectives so characteristic of Senate debate. "What do you want of him?"

"If the distinguished and able lady will yield to the distinguished and able gentleman who presently teaches at Stanford University," he said with the laughter in his voice that came when he felt he had really pulled a shrewd one, "I'll tell him. It has something to do with Charlie Macklin being too harsh on civil rights and too much of a law-and-order man for me. Get on the extension, if you like, and we'll talk it over together."

"I don't believe it," she said slowly but with a rising excitement, "I just don't believe it. *Mark!* It's Larry in Sacramento."

And from that moment until this triumphant one seven months later, Mark remembered as Linda shifted and murmured something unintelligible at his side, their lives had no longer been their own; a condition he now knew, with an odd mixture of elation and revulsion, would be permanent.

The announcement had taken the state by surprise.

"His sole merit appears to be a liking for yogurt which he shares with our casual governor," said the San Francisco *Chronicle.* "Mark Coffin, an extremely young man with no particular qualifications, wants to take his vast inexperience and his bag of Pampers to Washington," said the L.A. *Times.* But the governor, having made his decision, went all out. Three weeks remained in which to make Mark a statewide figure and if possible win him the nomination. The first step was to take leave from the university, which was granted willingly in the state of general campus euphoria created by the announcement of his candidacy. The second was to form a hasty campaign organization, largely composed of Stanford students, led by his favorite pupil, Johnny McVickers, a lanky, brilliant senior from Redding in Northern California. Most of them took leave, too, some officially, others informally: "Mark's Flying Squad" became an instant media favorite. The third step was to co-operate with the immediate novelty-interest that brought him exposure on all major state and national news and talk shows. Within ten days he had appeared on seventeen. And the fourth step was simply to slog up and down the state speaking at every possible appearance that could be arranged for him—one hundred twenty-three, they figured by primary day, reaching from Calexico on the Mexican border to Crescent City near the Oregon line; sometimes as many as eight or ten a day.

The sum total of all this was that when the primary votes were counted, Mark Coffin of Stanford had narrowly squeaked in between Charles Macklin of Los Angeles and the ex-governor. The first of my great overwhelming victories, he told himself now. That boy Mark Coffin is *really* a vote-getter!

Nonetheless, he *had* won the election, just as he

had today, and that was all that mattered. He had been suitably humble and earnest after the primary, and it had been quite genuine. "I've got a hell of a long way to go yet," he told his first press conference next morning; and truer word, he decided, he had never said. His opponent in the other party was also an ex-governor, also aging but possessed still of a tremendous force, vitality and attractiveness.

"You're going have to scramble, boy," Senator Elrod told him when he came out to join him for a week of campaigning in Orange County, where Jim's brand of conservatism could be of help in allaying fears that Mark might be "too liberal"; and scramble Mark did. For six months he rarely saw his home, rarely saw his children. He and Linda were on the road every day, all day and often far into the night. And her help, he acknowledged freely to everyone but most especially to her, was invaluable. Counseling, consulting, advising, she helped as only a child of politics, who wanted desperately to be back in it, could.

"Having been lucky enough to marry into the United States Senate," he would say when introducing her, "I now want to get there on my own. My greatest assist in this is known as Linda Elrod Coffin." There would be a tremendous roar of approval and welcome, Linda would step to the microphone and deliver a few gracious and charming remarks astutely aimed at the interests of whatever locality they happened to be in at the moment, and he would know he had added another thousand votes to his tally.

But California, as he sometimes remarked ruefully to Johnny McVickers, was a lot bigger than he had ever realized, when you saw it from the grass-roots level. At times it seemed to loom above him like some great elusive cloud he was never going to really penetrate.

"I feel I'm just skimming the surface," he remarked once in frustration to the governor.

"It always feels that way," the governor said, "but you just have to keep going. You'd be surprised how much filters down to influence the general judgment."

So he took fresh heart and went on; and gradually, in some instinctive way that he could not explain and did not reveal, he became convinced that he was getting through to the electorate, and would win. But he had never dreamed, of course, that his winning, narrow and photo-finish as it had been, would also carry with it a President of the United States.

That was a burden, he thought now with a sigh more worried than he wanted to admit, that Young Mark Coffin could very nicely do without, thank you. He had professed himself to be unconcerned about it earlier this evening, and his remarks to the President-elect had been far more respectful and humble than Linda and his immediate circle had desired; but how else was he to handle the handicap of having the nation's most powerful man feeling beholden to him? Inevitably it would make the President, for all Mark's meticulous respect and all the President's outward amicability in the moment of their mutual triumph, feel jealous and resentful. And having a jealous and resentful President at the other end of Pennsylvania Avenue was no way to begin a promising senatorial career.

The best thing for him to do, Mark decided now, was simply to continue the respectful attitude and try as best he could to go along with the President's programs. He did not anticipate too much trouble with this, because he really believed in what the President professed to stand for: honesty, integrity, candor, decency, good government, good appointments, an open, straightforward, imaginative, freedom-strengthening foreign policy—all the things, in short, that all Presidents stand for on the day they take office. The day after sometimes turns out to be a different matter, but as of now, Mark could see few problems, because in most fundamentals their campaigns had paralleled.

Both favored a liberal approach to the problems of government at home; both favored a policy of sensible accommodation abroad. Both were wary of big government, big military, big spending, big gestures abroad that couldn't be supported when the chips were down; both wanted honesty, integrity, candor, decency—et cetera. Both, in short, had fought the same campaign that American candidates of whatever political leaning almost always fight: the great Middle-of-the-Road, All-Things-to-All-Men, All-Purpose campaign that American voters want. Only very rarely did someone, a Goldwater, a McGovern, try anything really radical in either direction; defeat always resulted. In America the middle of the road was best, tried and proven in a hundred thousand campaigns from city council to White House. The really deciding factors were the nature of the candidate, the voters' understanding of him as a human being, and a slight gloss, either liberal or conservative, to suit the constituency.

Increasingly in recent years that constituency, after a lengthy period of relatively extreme conservatism, followed by an even lengthier period of relatively extreme liberalism, had returned to the middle ground of relative moderation. In ominous times, the national instinct seemed to be to close ranks and move back to the center. Questions of character and integrity, purpose and intent, vision or lack of it, became more important in the selection of leaders. It was there if anywhere, Mark knew, that he might face trouble with the new incumbent of the White House.

There, and possibly in the Senate as well. Because he knew, with a certain rueful self-knowledge, that underneath his own steady and easygoing exterior there beat a stubborn and determined heart. He really did believe, as he had declared to great applause many times in his campaign, in "getting rid of the old shabby deals of old shabby politics." He really did believe in fighting hard for his convictions in matters foreign and domestic. Arguments in the political science department at Stanford were a long way from arguments on the floor of the United States Senate. At school he had raised little fuss, made few enemies, engaged in little contention: the stakes, while important in their context, were not that great. They were as nothing to the stakes he would be dealing with now.

In the Senate he would have to speak up—he would be tested—and he would survive or go under. Whichever, he would try to do it honestly and with integrity if he could . . . *If he could.*

Could he?

He thought about this for a long time as he lay there in the dark; thought about all the challenges, and no doubt all the people, that were waiting for him in Washington, thought about it all so hard, in fact, that Linda finally stirred again, roused by some instinct responding to his mood. But her words were oblivious of the mood and filled with a great contentment.

"Oh, Markie!" she said, using the diminutive she only used in moments of greatest tenderness and intensity. "You've *won!*"

"Yes," he murmured, letting go at last, sleep beginning to come.

What, he did not altogether know.

3

Overnight the mood changed: there was no time left to brood or even think very much. Two months stretched between election and the convening of Congress on January 4. It seemed they vanished in a day.

For one precious week he took Linda and the kids and escaped to the fabulous home of an old friend, Frank Brandstetter, high above "Las Brisas" in Acapulco. There, surrounded by Brandie's generous hospitality and the attentions of his devoted staff, they lolled in the sun, did a little shopping, ate their meals in an airy gazebo on the lawn overlooking the entire sweep of the spectacular harbor; dreamed a bit, planned a bit, mostly just loafed. Their thoughtful host left them alone except when they sought his company at mealtimes, or for an occasional game of backgammon at the marble tables set along the edge of the enormous pool. They all turned brown, relaxed, unwound. Only Mark's parents and Jim Elrod knew where they were; for seven precious days the world did not get at them. On the eighth day they returned to Palo Alto and were swamped immediately in the great rush of preparation.

His first act next morning was to submit his resignation from the university. It was accepted at what turned into a public ceremony. The head of the department notified the *Stanford Daily* and the wire services; reporters and photographers descended upon the office, word quickly spread across campus. The dean, no slouch when it came to the uses of publicity, asked him to delay handing over his letter until the media had assembled. When all was ready he received it with a few ringing phrases he had obviously been polishing:

". . . express Stanford's pride in the sudden, sensational *and well-deserved* rise of one of her dearest sons . . . must pay tribute to his dedication to the university, to his students, to the cause of education itself . . . this great new calling worthy of his splendid talents . . . wondrous new opportunity to serve on national, nay, *world* stage . . . we are confident that . . . we *know* that . . . we all will watch with pride as he . . . honor . . . integrity . . . *decency* . . . Go, with Stanford's blessings!" Great applause and shouts from the hundreds of students who by now had gathered in the Quad. Again, "The Ax" and the Stanford Hymn. Again, clouded eyes and a real emotional wrench as he left the institution in which he had invested twelve of the happiest—in all probability *the* happiest—years of his life.

The days passed, then, in a blur of activity: congratulatory letters, telephone calls, telegrams, which he, Linda, Johnny McVickers and a corps of student volunteers did their best to answer; brief but well-publicized appearances up and down the state "to thank those who so generously and wonderfully gave me their support in this campaign"—an idea suggested by Senator Elrod, who had used it with great effect after his own much larger victories in North Carolina; return appearances on "Today," "Good Morning, America," "A.M. America," "Sixty Minutes," "Firing Line," the lot; interviews with the New York *Times,* the Washington *Post,* the wire services, most of the major dailies and magazines. In December *Time* gave him a cover story, just two weeks before the President-elect appeared in the same space as Man of the Year. The juxtaposition was too close for Mark's comfort, but he and the President exchanged hearty phone calls on both occasions, and what he was now beginning to regard as their truce was maintained unbroken in the public eye, though he felt with renewed uneasiness that it was being stretched to its limits by all the adulatory publicity heaped upon himself.

Through all of this, he and Linda tried, with considerable success, to keep their heads. "Don't forget you're not Young Mark Coffin," she would murmur wryly on some pompous occasion—"You're Humble, Homespun, Modest Young Mark Coffin." "I'm doing my damnedest," he would whisper back, "arrogant and difficult bastard though you know me to be." A secret amusement, a secret serenity—a secret singing—linked them together, both publicly and in private. It was his hour and Linda's, and it was obvious to a public that had decided to forget the closeness of the election and take them unanimously to its heart that they were riding high and loving every hectic minute of it.

During these weeks he received calls from a surprising variety of people in Washington. The first and probably the most important was Arthur Hampton of Nebraska, Majority Leader of the Senate, who called the day after his resignation from Stanford: a friendly call, interested, sympathetic, welcoming; not a trace of the political pressure, the gentle but unmistakable warnings that he was expected to get in line, which Mark had anticipated. Equally friendly, equally welcoming, equally noncommittal, was Herbert Esplin of Ohio, the Senate Minority Leader. Both told him to call them by their nicknames, and after a few seconds of hesitant formality he found it easy to do so. Both told him they expected great things from "the Senate baby"—"God, don't you hate that phrase?" Herb Esplin asked, sarcastically mimicking the media's use of it—and both promised all possible aid in helping him achieve "whatever it is you want to do here." This was the only point at which either gave any indication that he would like to know, and Mark parried them both with a laugh and an amiable "I'm really not sure what I want to do yet. I'll drop in when I get there and maybe you can tell me." Both chuckled at his reply and gave almost identical responses. "I expect you'll manage all right, whatever it is," Art Hampton said. "I have an idea you'll get wherever you want to go," Herb Esplin said.

I'm glad *you're* so confident, he thought as he hung up; but his own confidence was now building rapidly as a rising euphoria rushed him toward the day of his departure for Washington.

Another senatorial call came, this from a man who had scrupulously stayed out of the campaign and was now obviously trying to clamber aboard the bandwagon and make up for lost time: James Monroe Madison, senior United States Senator from California—with whom, Mark knew, he was now saddled for at least the four remaining years of Jim Madison's present term. He had never thought much of Jim Madison, and he didn't think much now, though he was scrupulously cordial and polite. He motioned Linda to pick up the extension, and they exchanged amused glances as Senator Madison fell all over himself expressing his pleasure and gratitude at Mark's victory. He, too, offered all possible help and assistance "as we work together for our great state," and Mark accepted it with a grave tone and a wink at Linda, in the spirit in which it was offered. "That will be interesting," he remarked when he hung up. "Very," Linda replied.

Another who called, almost immediately, surprising Mark with the warmth of his greeting, was Chauncey Baron of New York, the former Secretary of State who well-founded rumor indicated would be reappointed to that office by the incoming President. Secretary Baron also was most cordial—almost effusive, in fact, which hardly suited his rather icy public reputation. Mark was not ready to agree with Linda's quick question afterward—"What do you suppose *he* wants?" —but he had to admit he was a little puzzled by the call. More charitably after a moment Linda said: "I'll bet he expects you to be on the Foreign Relations Committee and is just building his bridges early."

"As a freshman, I don't have the slightest hope of being on that committee, as you very well know," Mark said.

"Don't give up the idea without a fight."

"I haven't even got the idea."

"Like fun," she said with a smile he had to respond to. "*Everybody* wants to be on Foreign Relations."

"I'm not going to even think about it. I'll be happier."

"*Ha!*" she said; and considered her hunch justified when, within a day, he also heard, out of the blue, from the British and French ambassadors in Washington.

Bright and cheery a few days later came another call. A surprisingly youthful feminine voice cried happily,

"Senator Mark Coffin! Am I really speaking to our most brilliant and surprising and amazing young politician in the whole big United States?"

"Yes, you are," he said, amused. "Who might this be?"

"Well, sir, this is Lyddie Bates. If you don't know who I am, just put your lovely young wife on the phone and she'll give me clearance."

"I know who Lyddie Bates is," he said, still amused. "I'll get Linda on the other extension."

"Well, children," she said when they were both listening, "I want you to come to a party for the President-elect the night of January fifth, the day after the Senate convenes. Can you come? You and Rick Duclos will be the only new senators there and there will be *lots* of important people for you to meet."

"Well—" Mark began hesitantly, but Linda cut him off.

"We'll be there, Lyddie. It will be absolutely delightful."

"Good!" she cried. "See you then, darlings. Black tie, of course!"

"Linda," he said a moment later, "are you really sure we want to get caught up in the social whirl quite that fast?"

"I've known Lyddie since I was ten," she said, "and *she* knows everybody who is anybody. It's imperative for us to be there if you want to get into the inner circle."

"Do I want to be in the inner circle?" he asked

moodily. "Do I really want to lose my independence that fast?"

"It's the only way to get things done," she said crisply. "Lyddie's offering you an entree that no amount of money could buy and I think she's an extraordinarily generous old dear to do it. I wouldn't think of not accepting."

"I'm glad *you* wouldn't," he said, more dryly than he intended. "I'm glad *somebody* in this family knows how to operate in Washington."

"Well," she said, flushing a little, "I do. I'm sorry if you think I'm pushy, Mark, but that's the way the game's played in Washington, and I intend for you to play it."

"I intend for me to play it, too," he said, softening his tone and taking her hand, "but I want to try to keep a few of my own rules intact while I'm doing it."

"I know," she said contritely, coming into his arms. "I shouldn't be so anxious, I guess. You know what you're doing. But it is *so* important to get off on the right foot."

"I'm doing fine so far," he said. "Don't worry." He cupped her chin in his hand and gave her the direct look of their most candid moments. "How are *we* going to play the game? What is Washington going to do to *us?* Do you ever think about that?"

"I think about it a lot," she said, her tone for a moment more worried than he knew she wanted to show.

"The big bad temptations of the big bad capital."

"They're there," she admitted. "I'm worried about them, for us and for the kids. But we're mature people and we'll just have to face them. All that matters is for you to do the things you can do."

"That doesn't matter more to me than my wife and my home," he said flatly.

"Remember that," she said, not quite as lightly as he knew she intended, "and everything will work out just fine."

"It will," he said soberly. "I give you my word on that. I've never done anything yet to hurt you or the kids, and I'm not going to now."

"Remember that," she said again, still not quite as lightly as she wished, "when you're in Washington, D.C."

"I will always remember that," he said again, as soberly as before. But the kiss with which they sealed it was just a little more desperate on her part than he would have liked for his own peace of mind, which as of then was quite honestly innocent of anything but the most absolute devotion to God, home, the flag and motherhood.

That, however was the only moment in the rush of days when anything at all interrupted the steadily rising tide of their confidence and happiness together; and when the governor called, as he did frequently—"Just to be sure I don't forget he has his brand on me," Mark said—"he thinks"—they were able to report cheerfully that all was going very well, that they were happy as clams and looking forward to doing "the great job you and the state expect of us," as Mark put it, giving it the priority he knew would please the governor. The governor did sound pleased and Mark was confident he would have his full support, and that they would agree on virtually everything when he took his seat in the Senate.

The days rushed on, narrowed down, suddenly spun out. Christmas and New Year's passed in a haze of farewell parties, appearances, interviews, good wishes. On January 2 they left San Francisco International Airport for Washington, D.C., seen off by a crowd of several hundred students, campaign workers, well-wishers, the media. His parents and the children preceded them into the plane; he and Linda turned at the top of the stairs for one last wave to the jubilant crowd jamming the waiting-room windows. A *Chronicle* photographer caught them with a zoom lens: handsome, happy, confident, excited, glowing. Ahead lay a marvelous journey to a marvelous culmination.

Mark's doubts were swept away in the euphoria of actually being on his way.

Washington had never seemed so exciting and enchanted. Washington would be all the things they had ever dreamed.

Never had they been so sure.

4

"The Everett McKinley Dirksen Senate Office Building," said the bronze plaque on the door as he paid the cabbie on a cold, snowy morning and turned to face his new home. Witty, florid, amiable, astute, always poking fun at himself even as he poked fun at others, a white-haired senatorial ghost cooed softly in his ear for a second, and vanished. "Oh, look!" a young secretary said loudly to her companion as they bustled up the steps ahead of him. "Isn't that Senator Coffin?" "He's *darling!"* her companion agreed with equal volume as they gave him their brightest smiles. He grinned and hurried forward to hold the door for them.

"Ladies," he said with mock gravity, "what a nice way to be welcomed to the Senate."

"Oh, Senator," the first said, "thank you so much. I'll have to tell Senator *Larson* I met you."

"And I'll have to tell Senator *McKendrick* I met you," said the other.

"And I," he said, chuckling, "will obviously have to visit both Senator *Larson* and Senator *McKendrick* and tell them *I* met *you.* What would be the best time to find you both in?"

"Oh, *Senator!"* they chorused, going off down the

hall convulsed with giggles, being careful to look back several times before they disappeared around a corner.

The amused smile that lingered from this brought him a lot of friendly smiles and greetings in return from hurrying Senate employees of both sexes as he walked along toward the elevator that would take him to the third-floor office Art Hampton had told him would be his. All down the long hallway he observed the signs of change, transition, continuity. Desks, chairs, sofas, lamps, boxes of books and bric-a-brac, pictures and paintings stood along the walls outside many doors. Movers were at work taking some articles in, taking others out, pushing loaded carts and dollies up and down the hall. The biennial game of musical chairs that members play with offices, using their seniority to have themselves shifted about to some favored location, some better spot, some place they conceive to be higher in the pecking order, was nearing completion on this day before the formal convening of the Congress. He only hoped his own office would be in some kind of reasonable order when he got there.

But of course it wasn't. Like many another, it still looked bare and gaunt; a few desks and typewriters, a sofa and chair or two, half-opened boxes, books and papers stacked against the walls, pictures of California scenes leaning against one another in a corner, telephones sitting on the floor at various outlets. Square in the middle was a huge senate desk, so far without its accompanying chair. Presiding over the chaos as the movers bustled in and out were two people: a pleasant-faced, slightly graying woman in her late thirties, fine features and dark coloring bespeaking her Chicano ancestry; a crew-cut boyish-looking, obviously efficient and obviously aware man, perhaps forty, who gave the impression of being very much in charge. These, he knew, must be the two he had asked to stay on, at least for the time being, from his predecessor's staff.

His impressions were instantaneous, possibly conditioned by what he had already gone through concerning these two. There was the slightest extra cordiality, not lost, he knew, upon the man, as he held out his hand to the woman and said,

"You must be Mary Frances Garcia from Los Angeles."

"Maria Francesca," she corrected with a smile, "but 'Mary Fran' to everybody. Welcome to Washington, Senator. This is Brad Harper."

"I assumed," he said, pleasantly, shaking hands with Brad, who returned the greeting with a cordiality that seemed a little forced, a certain nervous tension in his grip. "Nice to have you aboard, Brad. Nice to have you both aboard. I want to thank you very much for agreeing to stay on with me. It's going to help enormously to have both an experienced personal secretary and an experienced administrative assistant, right off the bat. I'd be lost without you."

"We're at your service, Senator," Mary Fran said.

"For the duration," Brad said.

"Or as long as you want us, whichever comes first, as they say in legislation," Mary Fran amended with a smile that carried just a slight edge. *I know who my ally is,* Mark thought; *and a good one to have. I can tell that already.*

"That's right," he echoed cheerfully, "whichever comes first. But I expect it will be quite a while before we have to decide that, won't it, Brad? After all, the governor was very insistent I keep *you* on; I don't see any reason why it shouldn't all work out very well. Don't you agree, Mary Fran?"

"Certainly, Senator," she said, voice noncommittal. "You already have some visitors from the press waiting for you in the inner office."

"Oh?" He smiled. "They *are* on the job early."

"These three always are," Brad said. "Watch out for them. They're sharp. Want me to come in with you?"

"I don't think that's necessary," he said. "I'll yell if I need help."

And with a wink at Mary Fran and a smile to Brad that deliberately robbed his comment of its sting—though not, he hoped, of its memory—he opened the door to his office and walked in. A comfortable, gray-haired man of sixty, a good-looking and obviously rather superior young man of twenty-eight, a sleekly stylish and very pretty girl of twenty-six, stared at him blandly.

"I'm Bill Adams of the AP," the older man said, holding out his hand.

"Glad to know you, Bill," he said, "I'm Mark Coffin. I believe I've met Chuck Dangerfield—"

"Once in San Francisco during the primary and a couple of times in Orange County during the campaign," Chuck said, looking pleased at being remembered. "How are you, Senator?"

"Fine. And your name is—?"

"Lisette Grayson of ABC," she said, giving his hand a strong, no-nonsense shake that didn't go at all with her beautifully feminine appearance. He made a note to remember this.

"Excuse me a minute while I get comfortable," he said, taking off his jacket, loosening his tie and rolling up his sleeves with a casual air he hoped would get them on his side at once. He was very well aware that in this, his first interview on the Hill, he must keep his wits about him. He had already discovered on a few occasions in California how easy it is to say something offhand that can be made to sound very foolish in print. The stakes now were even higher.

"Sorry we have no chairs yet," he said, seating himself casually on the corner of the big Senate desk, "but pull up some packing cases and we'll have at it. What can I do for you?"

"How does it feel to be here at age thirty, Senator?" Bill Adams asked. Mark turned promptly and looked behind him, then back, with a grin.

"I thought when you said 'Senator' that somebody was standing behind me. I'm not quite sure it's me, yet."

"It's you," Lisette assured him with obvious approval. Bill Adams snorted.

"I told you what I was going to say to him."

"Don't you dare!" she cried merrily, hitting him on the knee with her notebook. "I'll never speak to you again."

"What's that?" Mark asked.

"I said—"

"Bill!"

"I said I was going to warn you to look out for our Lisette, because she's dynamite."

"Strictly professional dynamite, Senator," she assured him. "I'm just here to get a story for ABC. What else would I be here for?"

"I'm here to try to give you one," he replied matter-of-factly, ignoring the question.

"Good," Chuck said. "Tell us whether you can work with the new President you elected in California."

"Well, now, wait a minute," he said with a comfortable smile. "Don't say *I* elected the new President in California. He elected himself. I was just along for the ride."

"The figures show the ride was the other way around, Senator."

"I couldn't have made it without him," Mark said firmly. "And call me 'Mark,' for God's sake. I'm young enough to be your son. Yours, anyway," he added to Bill as they all laughed.

"All right, Mark," Bill said. "What *are* you going to do here, then, be a yes man for him?"

For just a second Mark looked startled and annoyed; but he recovered very fast, because he knew he must get used to this kind of attempt to catch him off guard and provoke him into something quotable. His gaze was easy but his tone emphatic when he replied.

"I'm not here to be a yes man for anybody, Bill—not even you. Or you. Or you—" staring straight at the others. "I'm here to be Mark Coffin of California and do the best job I can—for the country, corny as that may sound—and for my state—and for the whole wide world, if I get the chance. Is that all right?"

"I think you've got your priorities correct," Bill Adams said. "It's nice to hear somebody around here be corny. If you can't be corny at your age, when can you? So you're not going to be a rubber stamp for him, hm?"

"No, I said I'm not," Mark iterated, this time permitting a little sharpness to surface. "Want me to write it out and sign it for you?"

"You do that," Bill replied, unabashed. "Then I can sell it back to you in a few months for a very handsome price."

"Never," Mark said flatly.

"Then we can expect you to oppose the President pretty consistently," Lisette said smoothly. Mark started to look at her with some exasperation, then shook his head with a sudden laugh.

"You guys have it all down pat, don't you? How to Put New Senators on the Spot and Watch Them Wriggle, with incidental courses on How to Create Friction Between the White House and the Hill. I can see it's the local art form."

"Some of us are better at it than others, Mark," Chuck said. "Personally, I don't go in for these games much. I'm just going to wait and see what you do."

"Noble you!" Lisette said. "How about giving us a general statement of your philosophy of government, Mark, and then maybe tomorrow morning, or day after, rather, since tomorrow's opening day and you'll be awfully busy, I can bring a camera crew in and we'll get it on tape for a special on 'New Faces in the Senate.' How would that be?"

"That would be fine," Mark agreed. "Well—" He paused and frowned while they waited expectantly. A couple of movers came in with a huge overstuffed leather chair, placed it behind the desk. He shifted to it.

"Now you can be properly senatorial," Bill said.

"It's wonderfully inspiring," he agreed. "Now, seriously"—and he did speak seriously and, he found to his satisfaction, without embarrassment—"let me put it this way:

"I've grown up through a fairly tough period in this country, civil rights, the unrest of the Sixties, Vietnam, Watergate, the whole bit. It's bound to have had an effect on me, as it has on all of us, particularly we who were growing up while it all went on. So for quite a while I was disposed to be very critical of our government and of what we were doing in the world. Without getting myself too radicalized about it, because that isn't my nature, I thought we were a lot of pious pretense without much substance, a lot of hot air concealing a pretty dank cesspool underneath.

"But after a while that began to change: I grew older and, I hope, more mature—though I guess at thirty" —with a deprecating smile—"I still have a long way to go. But anyway, I began to understand things a little better, to become a little more tolerant, to study my history a little more thoroughly, to realize how certain things developed, not always out of malice or deliberate evil intention but just out of men's incompetence, blindness, human error, avarice, stupidity. And I saw also that these were failings of free men—who were able to indulge themselves in failings just because they *were* free—and whose failings could sooner or later be caught up with and stopped, because they live in a free system with its own built-in correctives.

"And I began to perceive that America, for all her faults—and they are many—still has strengths and potentials that far out-balance them. The battle is, it seems to me, to make sure that the strengths *do* win out over the weaknesses. And basically, I think, all *that* requires is that we do the best we can to be always decent and tolerant, compassionate and kind toward one another; and that we try our best to be honest and straightforward in our dealings together; and that we do not lose sight of the fact that this democratic system is really just about the greatest marvel in all of human history, because it is the only system that allows free men to run their own government—*in their own way.* Nobody forces us—nobody dictates to us—we destroy only ourselves if we don't measure up. *It is up to us. We* are the government; and that, I think, is the most marvelous thing I know . . .

"This is what I believe. How I will translate it into action in the United States Senate, I do not yet know. But I will do my damnedest, of that you can be sure

. . . Now"—deliberately breaking the mood—"is that corny enough for you? I hope so, because it's me."

"It's quite sufficient for me, Senator," Bill Adams said, rising and shaking his hand, genuinely moved.

"And for me," Chuck Dangerfield said, doing the same.

"And for me," Lisette breathed, taking his hand between hers. "It's wonderful. *You're* wonderful. May I come back day after tomorrow and just hang around? To hell with 'New Faces in the Senate.' I just want to do a story on 'A New Senator's First Day.' "

"Always thinking," Bill Adams remarked. "Why don't you drop in on Joe McFadden of Massachusetts, who is a happily married Catholic of sixty-seven with ten children and thirty-three grandchildren? He's a *most* distinguished new senator. He'd be ideal for your story."

"Oh, hush," she said cheerfully. "I know where the glamor boy is. *You* aren't afraid of me, are you, Mark?"

"I don't think so," he said deliberately as he saw them to the door. "I think I can be brave. We'll see you day after tomorrow."

But after he closed the door he leaned against it and said, *"Whoooooosh!"* in a very thoughtful voice.

He did not have too long to think about it. In a moment the movers were knocking again, this time with additional chairs, a sofa, some end tables, lamps; his office was rapidly beginning to take shape. A familiar face appeared behind them: Johnny McVickers, just arrived in Washington to start part-time work in the office and get his master's in political science at Georgetown University. He was obviously afloat on a wave of excitement and idealism at the start of his Washington adventure.

"Johnny-boy!" Mark said, giving him a bear hug. "You got here safely. Did you have a good flight?"

"Great."

"Is your hotel room all right?"

"Sure. But I think I may have a roommate lined up."

Mark smiled.

"Already? Who is he?"

"His name is Pat Duclos."

"Oh—"

"Yes, the senator's son. Seems like a very nice guy. I don't think he likes his dad much, though—or maybe he does, I don't know, that's just a quick impression that may not be fair. But I think there's some trouble there. I didn't know who he was at first and I told him about you and what a great job you're going to do. He said he was going to work for a senator, too, but he was pretty cagey about it. Finally he said Rick Duclos of Vermont. I said I bet he was going to do a good job, too, and without telling me who *he* was, he said, 'Maybe. If he can keep his mind on his business.' Then when he finally told me his name it made me a little uncomfortable. But we agreed we'd think about sharing. I think it's too bad when a guy doesn't like his own father. That troubled me."

"That *is* odd," Mark said thoughtfully. "I like his father, from what I've heard of him. I expect he and I are going to become pretty good friends. Maybe we can help them."

"While we're saving the country," Johnny said with a sudden mischievous grin.

"That, too," Mark agreed with an answering humor. "So why don't you go out and get yourself familiar with the office buildings and the Capitol now, and Lin and I will see you later for dinner at Senator

Elrod's, O.K.? We're staying there for the time being until we can find a house."

"Sure thing. I can't wait to get started!"

"That makes two of us. Send in Brad Harper and Mary Fran Garcia, will you?"

"Yes, *sir!*" Johnny said, leaping to the door. "Mrs. Garcia! Mr. Harper!"

"How did the press treat you?" Brad inquired when Johnny had swung out, aglow with what seemed to be a permanently pleased and excited grin. "All right? They're a pretty tough bunch around here, particularly Bill Adams, who started on the Hill so long ago I believe he was a young reporter covering God's first term. I think it might be a good idea in the future if you let me sit in on interviews with you. It can save a lot of embarrassment later."

"You didn't do that with our last boss, Brad," Mary Fran said with an edge in her voice she didn't bother to conceal. "Why do you think you ought to do it with Senator Coffin? I didn't realize that was part of an administrative assistant's duties."

"It is if his senator wants it to be," Brad said with a certain smugness that indicated he thought Mark would agree. Mark did not.

"I don't know," he said easily, prompting an openly approving nod from Mary Fran. "I think maybe I can manage by myself. I'm a big boy, now—not a *very* big boy, but—thirty, anyway. I'll try it by myself for a while, and if it gets too tough I'll call you in. Tell me a little about yourselves, you two. What does a senator's administrative assistant do? What does a senator's secretary do? Hell, what does a *senator* do? You two have been in this California office for four years now. I need your help."

"First of all, Senator—" Mary Fran began. He raised a hand.

" 'Mark.' I know such familiarity breaks down discipline, but let's try it anyway. If you get too fresh I'll break out the blacksnake whip. In the meantime, relax."

"Thank you," she said, pleased. "In the first place, I think we both owe you great thanks for deciding to keep us on. It's usually customary for a new man to bring in an entirely new staff. I, at least, appreciate it very much."

"So do I," Brad agreed smoothly. "What makes you think I don't, Mary Fran?"

"I appreciate your appreciation, both of you," Mark intervened with equal smoothness. "Particularly you, Brad, because I understand you had some hopes of running for this office yourself. The governor commended you very highly to me [*virtually insisted I keep you,* he reminded himself privately, *though I'm damned if I know why, yet*] and said to tell you how much he appreciated your willingness to stay out of the primary. I appreciate it, too."

"That's the chance of the game, Senator—Mark," Brad said. "Sure, I would have liked to run, but who knows? I probably couldn't have won and I probably wouldn't have been a very good senator if I had. You've got the brains and the looks and the glamor: I think I can find real satisfaction in helping you. And anyway, there's Jim Madison, you know. He comes up in two years. Maybe I can take him on."

"You might have a chance," Mary Fran conceded, "though he's in so solidly it may take an atom bomb to blast him out. I don't know why exactly, either. He's such a pompous fool."

"California does seem to like him," Mark agreed, "and he *is* my senior colleague. And I am, incidentally, supposed to go and see him very shortly. So what do you have for me at the moment, anything?"

"Twelve applicants for office positions, tomorrow morning at nine," Mary Fran said.

"Do I have to see them all?" he asked, beginning to feel the first of what he knew would very soon become an avalanche of official pressures. "Can't you two decide?"

"I think you'd better see them," she said, "just in case you have to mediate."

"Surely not between you two!" he said with a smile, though it was obvious he would, and probably on many occasions, too. "What have you got for me, Brad?"

"The party caucus at ten-thirty. Better get there early. And don't talk to the press."

"For heaven's sake, Brad," Mary Fran said sharply. "Let the man make his own decisions!"

"The man will," Mark promised amicably. "Anything else for the moment?"

"Yes," Brad said stiffly. "A delegation of Girl Scouts from Anaheim will be in late this afternoon. You're to greet them for photographs on the Senate steps and sign autographs. After the caucus meeting tomorrow you'll of course be on the floor for your swearing-in, and then you have a lunch with the other new senators in one of the private dining rooms in the Capitol—I'll find out and let you know which one. Back to the session if it's still going, which it probably won't be, since the first day is mostly formalities. Then at three P.M., back over here, a group of farmers from the Central Valley, and after them a group of concerned citizens opposed to further defense spending. You'll tell them what you think."

"What do I think?" Mark couldn't resist asking, and Brad had the grace to look embarrassed. He also looked annoyed for just a second before he concealed it.

"Whatever you like, Mark," he said calmly. "I could make some suggestions, but you obviously have your own thoughts to express."

"Good," Mark said blandly. "I wasn't sure . . . Mary Fran"—sternly suppressing his urge to answer the amusement in her eyes—"is there anything else on your mind?"

"A few thousand congratulatory wires and letters already, which I'd suggest we answer with a form letter you can work out. We have a signature machine, you know. I'll get a new logo with your signature on it and we'll run them through."

"No," he said, "I think I'll sign these first ones myself. I don't want to start using phony gimmicks until I absolutely have to—which no doubt I soon will, for lack of time. But for now, let's let 'em have the Real Me. Anything else?"

"Yes, Lyddie Bates called to remind that you and Linda are coming to dinner with the President-elect tomorrow night."

"Ah, our famous hostess with the mostest."

"She's really a delightful old lady," Mary Fran said. "You'll love her. Hopefully, she'll love you. In fact, I know she will."

"Linda tells me this is very important."

"She can be a great help."

"Careers are made and broken at Lyddie's," Brad agreed. "Treat her right and she'll be your friend for life."

He grinned.

"I guess I can ride on my wife's coattails."

"She'll love you just for yourself," Mary Fran assured him, and suddenly looked flustered at her own earnestness.

"Well, thank you," he said with a smile that gently saved the moment. "Now I really must go and see

Jim Madison. And then I must stop by and pay a courtesy call on my father-in-law. Tell the President-elect," he added, joking, not really meaning it, "that I'll be back by five, if he calls."

"He may," Brad said. "He just may. I'll give him a message, if you like."

"Just that I'll be back by five," Mark said, grabbed his coat, shrugged into it and hurried out. Outside, not quite closing the door into the corridor, he paused and listened.

"Watch yourself, Brad," Mary Fran said coolly. "I have a feeling if you get too pushy our new man may push you right back."

"Which would please you, wouldn't it!" Brad snapped.

"I'd be absolutely delighted," she said, and sailed out to the reception room, not even noticing the slightly opened door as she passed. Through the crack he could see Brad standing beside the Senate desk, his face a study in anger and frustration. Currents and depths here, he told himself: Sailor, beware! He eased the door shut and went on his way, through still more corridors crammed with the clutter of restlessly migrating senators, to the office, in the old, tradition-hallowed Richard B. Russell Senate Office Building, of his senior colleague, the Honorable James Monroe Madison.

This, he told himself five minutes later, was a senatorial office that was a senatorial office. Busts and pictures were everywhere: big busts, little busts, big pictures, little pictures. Seven of the busts were of Washington, Jefferson, Lincoln, James Monroe, James Madison, Teddy and Franklin Roosevelt. Seven more, resting here and there in casual display, were of James Monroe Madison. Similarly, the photographs included a scattering of Senate colleagues. The rest were James Monroe Madison alone, James Monroe Madison with wife, two daughters, two sons-in-law, three grandchildren; James Monroe Madison with party leaders; James Monroe Madison with dog and cat; James Monroe Madison with foreign dignitaries; James Monroe Madison with subcommittee members inspecting redwood groves in California, oil and gas pipelines in Alaska, Israeli fortifications in the Sinai, Egyptian pyramids at Giza; James Monroe Madison with Presidents; James Monroe Madison against the Capitol, the Supreme Court, the White House—several of these, Rose Garden, Truman Balcony, East Portico, etc.

Two flags, that of the United States on one side, California on the other, flanked the high-backed leather chair in which sat that silver-topped edifice, the man himself, James Monroe Madison. When Mark entered he was living up to his cloakroom reputation, cruelly echoed from a famous senator of an earlier day, as "the only senator who can strut sitting down." But when Mark appeared he leaped to his feet and came forward with a bound, arms outstretched to clasp both of Mark's hands in his.

"Mark, my dear boy!" he exclaimed. "How marvelous to have you here! What a sensational introduction you have had to the Senate and to national life! How glad we all are to have you join our ranks as we work and strive for this great democracy of ours! And how glad *I* am to have such a young, vibrant, intelligent, and I may say *attractive*—oh, I hear the ladies are eying you already!—colleague to help me as I serve the people of Our Great State of California! Sit down, dear boy, sit down! *Helen!* Hold all calls until further notice, if you please! Mark and I must talk! . . .

"Well!" he said, resuming his seat at the desk while Mark, looking a trifle dazed, sat slowly down in the chair across. "What *are* your plans for California, my dear boy?"

"Why—" he began, and paused. "Why, just to do the best I can, I guess."

"And it will be ample, my dear boy, *ample,*" cried James Monroe Madison, "of that I am absolutely sure. But what I mean is, specifically, what about the new President's decision to appoint Charlie Macklin to be U.S. Attorney General?"

"Macklin!" Mark exclaimed. "Charlie *Macklin?"* For a moment his dismay was entirely apparent. Then he masked it with a determined effort and said cautiously, "I hadn't heard about that yet."

"You *hadn't?"* Senator Madison cried. "You mean he didn't consult the new junior senator before he—ah, well, you *are* new, *very* new, and so perhaps he felt that he would discuss it with me first and *then* tell you. I'm sure he will—I'm *sure* he will. Probably before the day is out, I suspect. It would be a great discourtesy to you not to. After all, one *does* consult senators from a state before appointing someone from that state. I mean, *I* would, as all sensible Presidents *do.* So I'm sure he will. Anyway, what do you think about it?"

"Well, I thought," Mark said, still very cautiously, "that one of the reasons for choosing me for the nomination instead of Charlie Macklin was that Charlie had been too rough on civil liberties when he was district attorney of Los Angeles County, and also that his stand on civil rights was perhaps a bit—inflexible, shall we say. Or am I mistaken?"

"Oh, I—I don't know whether you're mistaken or not, Mark. I really don't. There may have been other reasons, probably there were dozens. Was that your impression, that that was why you were selected? That good old Charlie has been too much law-and-order and racist, as it were, as the popular phrase has it?"

"You know he has," Mark said levelly, beginning to recover a bit. "You know exactly that he has. Are *you* going along with his appointment?"

"Well, now," Jim Madison said, clasping his fingers together and staring at Mark solemnly over them. "Well, now, let's see. We must consider these things very carefully, of course. We must look at all the angles, both those affecting California and those affecting the United States; and, of course, our image in the world, which is also very important. But above all, of course, we must look at what Our Great President wants, mustn't we, now. Musn't we!"

Mark fixed him with a solemn and unimpressed eye.

"Must we?"

"Well, now, my dear boy, my dear boy! Surely you know—surely you understand—surely in your own brilliant studies of the American government, you yourself know and have stated that a President's party members, barring the most *extreme* reasons of conscience, are really expected to go along with him, now, they really are! You don't want to begin your Senate career by opposing your own President, do you? To say nothing of the governor—"

"*What?* I don't believe it!"

"Yes, the governor," Jim Madison said solemnly. "Oh yes, oh yes. I understand that he also is most anxious for this appointment to be approved. So you would be opposing both your President *and* your governor, Mark. That would be a frightful error! California would never forgive you! The governor would never forgive you! HE would never forgive you. Oh no, Mark. I can't let you do that. I simply can't!"

For several moments Mark did not reply. When he did it was in a grim tone of voice.

"I'll worry about California, and I'll worry about the President—and the governor too, if I have to. But I may not let that stop me when it comes time to vote on dear old Charlie Macklin." He stood up abruptly. "Is that all you wished to see me about? I don't mean to be rude, but I do have to stop in and see my father-in-law also, so perhaps if you'll forgive me, Senator—"

"Oh, *Mark!* Mark—Mark—*Mark!* I—is this what you want me to tell the President-elect and the governor? That you're going to oppose Charlie, our old friend Charlie? It may put us in opposition to each other, you know. Because I may—I may have to go along, you know. I *like* old Charlie, for one thing, and also, if Our Great President and Our Great Governor want him—there *is* such a thing as party loyalty, you know!"

"I know that," Mark said evenly, "but I'm going to think about it pretty carefully."

"Then you *do* want me to tell him—"

"If he asked you to sound me out instead of coming to me direct," Mark said, his anger, dismay and bewilderment finally spilling over into his voice, "then you tell him I am damned annoyed about it and I may or may not support his nominee. *That's* what you can tell him. Take care, Jim. I'll see you around."

And he shook hands brusquely with a seemingly flustered Senator Madison and stalked out. But Senator Madison was not really all that flustered.

"Ah, youth!" he said with a curiously pleased little smile, lifting the receiver and preparing to dial. "Ah, silly, headstrong youth. *Hah!*"

* * *

Silly he did not feel, but headstrong he certainly looked as he strode down the corridor, this time glancing neither to right nor left, exchanging no greetings, his face a study that caused some comment, to the nearby office of James Rand Elrod, senior senator from North Carolina, chairman of the Senate Armed Services Committee.

There he found Linda with her father. She kissed him with great warmth and stood back to survey him with satisfaction as he made his expression suitably bland to meet her experienced scrutiny. He expected her to detect his concern but he found at once that she had concerns of her own.

"Who is this scarlet woman I hear is going to be in your office all day?" she asked lightly—lightly but prepared, he could see, to become more serious if she felt she had to.

"What?" he demanded, sounding annoyed for a second but managing a quick change to a wryly amused smile.

"You'll learn," Senator Elrod said comfortably. "Who is it, that little Grayson girl?"

"How did you know?" he asked, taking a chair and acting more at ease than he really felt, suddenly.

"She goes after everyone," Jim Elrod said, "particularly the young ones. They're always such good subjects for her special interviews, she says. I suspected she'd be after you, first thing."

"She is," Mark admitted, "but"—turning to Linda—"how did *you* know?"

"A little bird told me," she said, again lightly but obviously still prepared to do battle if necessary. "A little bird named Lisette. She saw me in the hall on my way over here and sailed right up to me. 'I'm going to borrow your husband for a day,' she told me. 'I hope you don't mind.' "

"And do you?" he inquired, while her father looked increasingly concerned. She gave him an appraising glance.

"I don't quite know, yet. Should I?"

"Linda! For God's sake, what *is* this nonsense?"

"You just watch out for her, that's all," she said, still trying to pretend she was being humorous but getting the little strain lines around her mouth that he knew very well. "Maybe I'd better come along to keep you company."

"You certainly will not!" he said, more strongly than he intended. "You'd make me feel like a damned kid. Stop worrying! She's just a reporter out to get a story. I've had her type in class—they always want to stay after and talk to teacher."

"And have they?"

"Sometimes," he said calmly. "But that's all they've done. I repeat, Linda—stop acting like this. I'm all right. She's all right. The staff will chaperone me, I'll make sure of that. What's the problem?"

She gave him a suddenly sad and thoughtful look —where in the world was the confidence with which they had discussed this, just a few weeks ago?—and said slowly,

"This is Washington, D.C., and you don't know it, and I do. And I'm saying, watch out! I don't intend to be a Capitol Hill widow and don't you forget it, Mark Coffin!"

"Honey!" he protested, rising and taking her in his arms as he realized that she was now in deadly earnest. "Honey, honey! For *goodness'* sake, stop this. Stop it!"

For a long moment they stared intently at one another; then she yielded and moved deeper into his arms.

"I'm sorry," she said against his chest. "But I know this town and it—it *does* things to people. I don't want it to do anything to us, that's all."

"But just a while ago—a month or so," he said, bewildered, "you weren't so worried about this. You said—"

"We weren't here then," she said fiercely. "I don't want Washington to ruin *us,* that's all."

"It won't," he promised solemnly. "It won't ever do anything to us."

After several moments, during which he exchanged a troubled glance with his father-in-law, she released him and returned slowly to her chair. Jim Elrod cleared his throat with a loud "A-hem!" and said heartily,

"Well, Mark, how y'all likin' it here this first day around the United States Senate? Kind of excitin', isn't it?"

"Bewildering, I'd put it," Mark said with a cautious smile. Then his expression darkened.

"I've already learned that the President-elect, whom I thought I could trust, in co-operation with the governor, whom I also thought I could trust, is going to nominate a man for Attorney General whom I don't honestly think I can support—Charlie Macklin," he responded to Linda's suddenly alert and questioning look, and she said sharply, "Oh no!"

"Yes," he said grimly, "and he didn't even consult me on it, either."

"The man comes from California?" Senator Elrod asked, surprised.

"Yes, he's former D.A. of Los Angeles County. Very uptight law-and-order type. Very rough on civil liberties, civil rights, sex, race. Too much for me, I think, although I suspect"—he smiled at his father-in-law—"you may like him."

"Yes," Jim Elrod said, "it's possible. But that does put you in a bind, doesn't it? Kind of rough for a brand-new senator to oppose a brand-new President of his own party. Are you sure you're goin' to do it?"

"I'm not positive yet. But it's going to take a lot of convincing to persuade me to go along."

Senator Elrod gave him a shrewd glance.

"And I suppose it'll take a lot of convincin', too, to persuade you to support the new defense bill I'm goin' to put in, won't it?"

Mark's expression became cautious again.

"What's it going to be?"

"An authorization to increase the defense budget by ten billion dollars," Jim Elrod said crisply. "At once."

"But why?" he demanded. "Why? I don't understand."

"Because the Soviet Union is buildin' up so fast that if we don't get busy pretty damned soon, we're goin' to be so far back there that they'll be able to blackmail the world at will—includin' us—and we won't be able to stop 'em, that's why."

"I don't believe it," Mark said stubbornly. "I just don't believe it. We have plenty of power to stop them any time."

"I beg to disagree."

"O.K., disagree, but you aren't going to convince me that we don't have such an atomic arsenal—"

"The will, Mark! *The will to bluff with it if we have to. The will to use it if we have to.* That's what we don't have, and they know it. So all the while they're lullin' us into thinkin' A-bombs are the answer to everythin', they've been buildin' up their Navy and their Air Force and their Army and all their submarines and missiles and rockets to the point where we're just about outgunned right this very minute.

They wouldn't expect us to use atomic weapons on 'em—they'd go for our throats with conventional weapons. That's where we're weak. That's where we've got to build up, and damned fast. That's why I'm puttin' in my bill. I'd like to think my son-in-law would support me on it, but I expect he won't—though I'd hope he'd at least do me the courtesy to listen to my arguments when we get to debatin' it."

"That I will do, Jim," Mark pledged soberly. "But, as with Charlie Macklin, it's going to take a lot of convincing . . ." His eyes suddenly widened. "Lord! Some first day around the U.S. Senate for me, I'd say. Two biggies I've got to worry about, right off the bat. Is it always like this?"

"It never stops," Jim Elrod said cheerfully. "Got to be tough around this place to stand the gaff. It never lets up."

"I hope I'll be tough," Mark said, still soberly. "I hope I'll be a good United States Senator. I'm certainly going to try."

"You will be," Senator Elrod said comfortably. "You've got a lot to learn, but I think you'll get there . . . Excuse me," he said, picking up his phone as a buzzer sounded. "Yes, ma'am, he's here . . . Yes, I will . . . Right away? . . . All right. He'll be comin' back there in just a minute. Thank you . . . Your office. The President-elect called and wants you to return it when convenient. No, hurry, I gather—just like yesterday mornin', perhaps. You can do it from here if you like, Linda Rand and I'll clear out."

"No, thanks," he said, "I'll go back to my own office. Want to come, honey?"

"Thanks," she said, "but I've got to get back to Daddy's place and give the kids an early supper. They're exhausted from all the excitement. And tomorrow we all have to be in the gallery when you're sworn in . . . And the day after that," she added almost defiantly, "we have to go house-hunting. All day."

"Why don't you wait until the weekend when I can go with you?" he suggested mildly. "Come spend the day with me instead."

"No, I can't do that now. You don't want me."

"Oh, honey!" he said in a voice more exasperated than he intended. "I was just kidding."

"Not exactly. Anyway, we've got to get settled just as soon as possible. We can't impose on Daddy any longer."

"Well . . ." he said slowly, and then decided to drop it. "O.K. Jim, I'll be thinking about your bill." He shook his head again. "Two big problems . . . See you later, honey. I've got to run and talk to the Man."

"Give him my love," Jim Elrod said wryly as he hurried out. "I don't think *he's* exactly goin' to like my bill, either . . ."

For a moment he and Linda stood looking at one another. Then he said gently,

"He thinks he's got two big problems, darlin'. Don't give him a third."

"I'll try not to, Daddy," she said, holding herself under tight control, "but I'm scared of this town. I know it—and I'm scared."

"I'm glad to see," he said to Mary Fran as he entered his own door—already, he noted, it felt like a haven from all the things that were about to descend on Young Mark Coffin, senator from California—"that we're beginning to look a little more inhabited."

"Since you left they've brought in more desks,

more sofas, some lamps, chairs, file cabinets—we're getting there."

"Soon we'll be calling it home. I understand I have a phone call to answer."

She nodded.

"He seemed quite insistent. Shall I get him for you?"

"Please. I'll take it at my desk."

In a moment a voice calm, firm and confident sounded cheerily in his ear.

"Mark!" it cried.

"How are you, Mr. President?" he responded calmly. "What can I do for you?"

"First of all, Mark, congratulations again on your splendid victory and on being here. I'm counting on you to be my good right arm in the Senate."

"You'll have a lot of them, Mr. President. I'll just be one among the many."

"But a very vital and important and irreplaceable one, I know . . . Mark, I want to talk to you about this appointment for Attorney General."

"Good," he said, a slight edge coming into his voice. "I understand you've already discussed it with my colleague."

"Only because he's your senior in the Senate, Mark. One has to use a lot of protocol with you boys, you know. It's like trying to find a basketball in a herd of elephants. You have to be *very* careful not to step on anyone's toes."

"Hearing the news first from Jim Madison might be considered such," Mark said evenly. "But of course," he added quickly, "I do see your problem. Anyway, Mr. President, I'm sorry—but I have a lot of reservations."

"Sure you do, Mark. Sure you do! You wouldn't

be a good senator—and you're going to be a *very* good one—if you didn't have. Why don't you come down to the hotel and discuss it with me? How about tonight?"

"I can't tonight. I've got to get home to Linda and the kids or she'd shoot me. We're staying with my father-in-law, you know, and she's got to go house-hunting and so on—lots of problems involved in getting settled." A genuine amusement came into his voice. "That's where you're lucky. You and George Washington *know* where you're going to sleep."

"Yes"—a happy chuckle—"that *is* one advantage of the job I hadn't really thought about, though I know Elizabeth has. Well, then: I hope you won't take any extreme positions on Charlie Macklin until we can talk. I won't announce the nomination until we have. You aren't going to be at Lyddie Bates' for dinner tomorrow night, by any chance? I think we'll be there if I can get away. It would be a nice informal place for us to slip away and talk for a minute without attracting too much attention. This place down here is swarming with media anyway: probably wouldn't be wise to do it here. Will you be at Lyddie's?"

"We've been invited, yes. I think we'll try to make it. She sounds like a delightful old gal."

"Lyddie's a love. Everybody's favorite Washingtonian, and that's quite a tribute. Let's see each other there, then, and maybe we can find a quiet place to talk. Lyddie will arrange it if I give her the word. All right?"

"All right, Mr. President. But I must warn you that I do *not* like this appointment and I'm going to find it very hard to go along with it."

"Let's talk, Mark. No arbitrary decisions now. Let's talk. I'll see you at Lyddie's."

"Yes, Mr. President, but . . ."

"Take care, Mark. Must run. The press awaits."

Click, and that was that. He frowned thoughtfully as he put the receiver slowly down. No sooner had it made contact than Mary Fran buzzed him.

"Yes?"

"Lisette Grayson. Shall I—"

"No," he said, trying to keep his tone impassive, though to his annoyance he felt himself tensing a little inside. "Put her on."

"Hi," she said cheerfully. "Are you exhausted from your first day in the great big U.S. Senate?"

"Oh, hello," he said, deliberately noncommittal. "Where are you?"

"Over here in the Senate television gallery feeling lonesome. What are you doing?"

"Getting ready to go home."

"To the wife and kiddies?"

"To the wife and kiddies."

She laughed.

"Well, all right. Don't sound so belligerent about it. I just asked. It's perfectly normal to go home to the wife and kiddies."

"And is it normal to call a United States Senator at the end of the day and tell him you're over in the gallery feeling lonesome?"

"I do it all the time."

"Yes, I'll bet."

"Now, now, don't believe all those naughty things you hear about me. My colleagues are just jealous. Has it been a hard day?"

"Rather, but exciting."

"O.K., I won't keep you. Do we still have our date for the story?"

"That was the agreement. I'll be here from eight-thirty on. My secretary, Mary Fran Garcia, will bring you in."

"And stick around every minute, I'll bet."

"I hope so."

"Mark, Mark! You're *impossible.*"

"Yes, I am," he said calmly, "so don't try too hard."

"Oh boy! Talk about senatorial dignity."

"Good night, Lisette. See you day after tomorrow, if you care to come by."

"Would you mind if I didn't?"

"I can see I'm going to be a very busy man in this place, and I don't really think I'd care one way or the other."

"Really?"

"Really."

"O.K., Mark. Pleasant dreams."

"You, too," he said cheerfully, and rang off; though he did not, if truth were known, really feel all that cheerful. He stood for a long moment at his desk, staring off into distances filled with presidential appointments, defense bills—and other things.

"Girl Scouts!" Brad said, popping his head in the door.

"I'll be right there," he said; put on his public face and an overcoat, and found his way through the corridors, subways, and elevators to the snow-covered steps on the Senate side of the Capitol. The faded blue of winter sunset was beginning to descend, the floodlights had been turned on the dome, the flag snapped briskly in the cold wind whipping off the Potomac. Rosy-cheeked, shivering and excited, the Girl Scouts from Anaheim clustered around him like little sparrows.

Amid much chattering, pushing, shoving, giggling and squealing as harried adult guardians tried vainly to maintain order, he patiently sighed autographs while a photographer snapped away: his first public duty in Washington, he thought wryly. And not such a bad one, at that, if you thought of Young Minds, Molding Our Youth, The Future of Our Democracy and all the rest of it.

"Senator," the photographer suggested finally, "why don't we get a group shot of all of you now, and then we can call it quits."

"Fine," Mark said. "We're all freezing to death, aren't we, girls? Why don't you line up on each side of me now—"

"All right!" the photographer cried. "Everybody say 'cheese.' "

An obedient chorus of "cheeses."

"One more, just to be sure. Get in a little closer to the senator, girls. He won't bite."

"That's right," Mark smiled, breath white against the chilly air. "I won't."

Flash, squeals, giggles: picture-taking over.

As he started to turn away one little girl about Linnie's age came up to him and took his hand with an innocent earnestness.

"Senator Coffin," she said, "is it *fun* to be a senator?"

For just a second he hesitated. Then the public grin grew wider.

"You bet it is," he said. "You bet it is!"

But as their adults shepherded them giggling and squealing away, he found himself staring upward very thoughtfully at the great Capitol dome outlined against the deepening sky; and the grin faded.

5

The Senate Majority Leader had a familiar, faintly melancholy thought as he surveyed the packed public galleries, the familiar faces in the media galleries, the bustle of aides, assistants, secretaries, senators, and Senate functionaries on the floor—*well, here we go again.* His twelfth session of Congress: twenty-two years to date, a long time out of a man's life. Twelfth session, fourth new President, one more "freshman class" about to take the oath of office and embark upon the duties of what its members liked to call "the world's greatest deliberative body." "It may not be the greatest," Alben Barkley had remarked in the midst of a filibuster against some New Deal measure, "but it's certainly the most deliberative."

And so, of course, it should be. Art Hampton, successor to Alben, Lyndon, Mike and many another in the long history of the office of Majority Leader, would not have it any other way, no matter how it frustrated him sometimes. He expected it would frustrate him this session, too: but, like his predecessors and most of his colleagues, he loved it. He wouldn't be anywhere else doing anything else—except possibly the White House, and that dream was long gone for him.

Here on the Hill was where so much of it all happened, anyway. He had seen Presidents come into office convinced they were now in command of everything, only to see them develop into sadder, wiser and suddenly much older men as they realized that they were not alone in the exercise of power. The Senate, the House and the Supreme Court had a lot to say about it too—particularly, senators liked to think, the Senate. Some Presidents had to take more bumps than others before they accepted this. Some were sophisticated enough politically and knowledgeable enough historically so that they accepted it at once and slid easily into the pattern of give-and-take between White House and Hill from which the nation's government emerged.

As he smiled and waved to familiar faces in the galleries—Chauncey Baron was there; Lyddie Bates, rosy and bright—"haven't missed an opening in thirty years"—sitting with Linda Coffin, the Coffin children, Mark's parents; such press friends as Bill Adams of the AP, Chuck Dangerfield of "Washington Inside," that morally indignant and professionally ruthless column, Lisette Grayson of ABC; Sir Harry Fairfield and Pierre DeLatour, the British and French ambassadors, old friends and astute judges of the Congress—Art Hampton wondered what this new President would do. He had been a successful governor of his state, a frequent visitor to Washington to testify before congressional committees on matters of import to it, but essentially he was an unknown. Only those who came from the halls of the Congress itself were known to Washington; and even they, once they moved into the Oval Office and began to see the world from the peculiar perspective of 1600 Pennsylvania Avenue, were not as known as old friends thought they were. They all developed presidentitis in some form or another. Art Hampton only hoped this one would not have too bad a case of it. If so, the Majority Leader would have more problems than usual steering administration bills through the Senate.

Because, he could tell, it was not going to be a very manageable Senate this session. Herb Esplin, his jolly side-kick who sat across the aisle from him as Minority Leader, might only have twenty-seven members on his side but he was a very shrewd manipulator when the majority was divided; and this time, with an unusually large total of twenty-three newly-elected senators, the majority might be more divided than it had been in quite some time.

Twenty-three new senators: he had called them all after election, a standard practice of his, welcoming them to Washington and the Senate, wishing them well, offering his help in whatever they needed to get them settled and make them part of the club. He had a friendly impression of most of them; because he was a fatherly soul who missed his late wife and the children they had always wished for and never had, he was especially drawn to the younger ones. Of these the ones that intrigued him most were Rick Duclos of Vermont, Bob Templeton of Colorado and the one everybody was interested in, young Mark Coffin of California.

Looking about the floor as returning senators shook hands and greeted one another effusively while the big clocks over the doors moved toward noon, Art Hampton observed that none of the freshmen were visible at the moment. They were, he knew, in the majority and minority cloakrooms just off the floor, waiting to come out and take the oath when the session began; greeting one another with the nervous, exhilarated excitement he could still remember from his own first day in the Senate. There was nothing like it, that keyed-up feeling that you were about to step on the national stage; it was one of the special once-in-a-lifetime feelings. After that moment, it was still exciting and still challenging but, like anything, it slipped fast into routine; it was never quite the same again. He envied them for a wistful second; to be young and about to become a United States Senator. No wonder it made him feel fatherly.

He was not too sure, from what he had heard of Mark Coffin, and from what he knew of Linda Rand Elrod Coffin, that Mark would want the fatherly assist he was prepared to offer. Certainly Linda had known her way around Washington from childhood. And his impression of Mark was that there was something there very solid, very self-contained, very self-reliant: a certain inward confidence that did not need other people—or thought it did not. Art Hampton was not quite sure where or how he had received this impression, but as a shrewd judge of political animals from all his years among them, he was pretty sure he was right about it. This could mean, for him and for young Mark Coffin, problems.

The Senate was the home of compromise, the fount of compromise, the citadel of compromise. It wore down those who refused to compromise. With some the process took longer than it did with others, but in time it conquered them all—if they wanted to stay, and if they really wanted to accomplish anything in the Senate. Mark Coffin, he was sure, wanted to stay a long time; and he sensed that he wanted to accomplish a great deal. Which was fine: Art wanted to help him, provided Mark did not make it too difficult for him.

He hoped, as the clocks stood at ten to twelve and the noisy excitement mounted in the galleries and on the floor, that this would not be the case. But he couldn't claim to be sure.

Behind the swinging glass doors that open from the Senate chamber into the majority cloakroom, no such uncertainties at this moment troubled the about-to-be junior senator from California. His moods, which had fluctuated so since his election—very unlike one whom everyone, including himself, had always considered so steady—were temporarily wiped out in the great euphoria that engulfed him. They might return soon—he expected they would—but right now he was simply so swept up in the excitement of the occasion that there was no room for them. It was here at last, the moment that would confirm his victory and his future. Amid a swirl of freshman senators nervously awaiting their ceremony, none was more quick-smiling, eager, excited, vibrant and alive than Mark Coffin of California, keyed up by the thrill of the day and the knowledge that he was about to take his place permanently in the history of his country.

In the midst of learning a fact about his new institution—that senators are the most handshaking people in the world, equally effusive whether they have seen one another a week, a day or one-half hour before—he found himself turning away from the older senators, who looked in from time to time to introduce themselves with cordial smiles and welcoming words, to bump into a much younger one, dark, charming, quick-smiling like himself.

"Hi!" the other said, holding out his hand before Mark could apologize. "I'm Rick Duclos of Vermont. They tell me we're going to be sitting beside each other when we get our desk assignments."

"Are we?" Mark responded with a pleased smile, shaking hands. "For many, many years, I hope. I'm Mark Coffin of California. I'm delighted to know you. Do you snore? They tell me senators sometimes do."

"I doubt if I will for quite a long time," Rick said with a grin. "I'm too excited at being here. But if I do, just give me a jab and wake me up."

"You likewise. I'm really delighted to know you."

"And I you. It's a great big wonderful Senate, isn't it?"

"It *is* wonderful," Mark said, his voice suddenly genuinely awestruck. "It's just wonderful being here."

"Now, there," said a hearty voice accompanied by a hearty chuckle, "are two freshmen with the right attitude." A huge good-looking Polynesian confronted them, hand outstretched. "Hi, I'm Kalakane Tokumatsu of Hawaii. They usually call me Kal. Or sometimes Toke. Or sometimes 'you half-Oriental son of a bitch,' depending on the mood. Anyway, welcome to the U.S. Senate."

And he gave them both a big, enveloping handshake and an exuberant hug, beaming down upon them.

"Great to know you, Senator—" they began simultaneously.

" 'Kal,' I said, damn it. There are a few old birds around here you'd better call 'Senator' for a while, but most of us you can call by our first names right away. And even the inner circle mellows pretty fast. After all, we're all in this together."

"Thanks, Kal," Mark said. "It's a help to know that."

"Help you any time," Kal said comfortably. "And you, too, Rick. After all, Hawaii's right next door to California, right? And Vermont, too, right?"

"Right," Rick agreed. "One nation, indivisible."

"That's right," Kal said, adding with a sudden laugh, "Except when we get in a few fights about things, now and then. But what the hell, we're human. You've no idea how human this Senate is, but you'll find out . . . Say, isn't that Bob Templeton over there, the guy who just lost his wife and two kids?"

On the other side of the room a sober-faced young man was shaking hands with a couple of equally sober-faced older senators.

"I believe it is," Mark said.

"What a hell of a thing," Rick said softly.

"It sure is," Kal agreed. He caught Bob's eye, waved him over. Almost defiantly, daring them to be sympathetic, Bob came.

"Hi," Kal said. "I'm Kal Tokumatsu of Hawaii. You're Bob Templeton, right?"

"I think everybody knows that," Bob said with a sad smile, shaking hands.

"Well," Kal said, touched but managing to stay hearty, "you're at home here. This is Mark Coffin of California, and this is Rick Duclos of Vermont . . . I've just been telling them that they're showing the proper awe and respect for this great institution you all are about to join today. I trust you have the same respectful spirit, Bob."

"Absolutely," Bob said, managing a stronger smile. "What do we have to do for you older guys, shine your shoes?"

"Make the beds, scrub the floors, do the dishes—you'll find out!"

A bell rang, long and steady. Kal put a finger to his lips, gestured them toward the swinging glass doors, and the floor.

"Twelve noon," he said. "School's in! Time to be dignified U.S. Senators now!"

He stood aside with a fatherly air to let them pass, and they were on the floor of the Senate. Instantly the tumultuous chamber quieted, a tense, excited hush fell over all.

"The Senate will be in order!" the outgoing Vice-President cried in this, one of his last official duties before preparing to leave office to make way for the new administration. "The chaplain will deliver the prayer."

Briefly the chaplain did so, invoking the blessing of Providence upon "him who is soon to lead our Nation, and these Your servants in the United States Senate, both old and new, who will assist him in the awesome task."

"Will the new senators please come forward to be sworn," the Vice-President directed. "The Senator from California!"

On the majority side of the aisle, Jim Elrod rose.

"Mr. President!" he said. "My very good friend and colleague, the distinguished senior Senator from California, has very graciously agreed to step aside today and let me escort his new colleague to the Chair to be sworn. May I present my son-in-law, Mark Coffin, junior Senator from the State of California!"

"The Senator will be sworn," the Vice-President said. Jim Elrod stepped forward, offered his arm; Mark had a blurred impression of many faces above, all smiling down upon him from a sea of applauding hands, Linda's face and the children's brightest and proudest of all. Then Jim was propelling him forward, they were walking slowly together down the aisle, he was about to become a United States Senator.

They reached the well of the Senate, he turned a face at once solemn, proud, thrilled and apprehensive to the Vice-President, who smiled benignly upon him and raised his right hand. "Raise yours!" Jim whispered, and he did so, afraid it would tremble, proud of himself when it did not.

"Do you, Mark Coffin," the Vice-President said, "solemnly swear that you will support and defend the Constitution of the United States against all enemies, foreign and domestic; that you will bear true faith and allegiance to the same; that you take this obligation freely, without any mental reservation or purpose of evasion; and that you will well and faithfully discharge the duties of the office on which you are about to enter; so help you God."

"I do," Mark said solemnly. "That's Daddy!" Linnie cried in a clear, penetrating voice from the gallery; and amid a burst of friendly laughter and applause the Senate welcomed its youngest member.

"The Senator from Colorado!" the Vice-President said as Mark and his father-in-law stepped aside to watch Bob Templeton come slowly down the aisle on the arm of his senior colleague.

"Well, you're here!" Jim Elrod whispered in his ear.

"Yes," he whispered back, a triumphant singing in his heart that temporarily submerged all else. "I'm here!"

6

"Is it always like this at Lyddie's?" he asked Linda and his father-in-law at quarter to eight that night as he jockeyed Senator Elrod's Chrysler into the long line of cars and chauffeured limousines inching around the curved drive toward the beautiful white house, floodlights streaming out on the snow, trees still lighted for Christmas, a mansion in a dream.

"Always," Linda said, a happy excitement in her voice. "Lyddia loves to entertain—it's always such fun to come here."

"You're pleased to be back, aren't you?" he asked, squeezing her gloved hand.

"It *is* nice," she agreed. "It's been two years since I've been to Lyddie's."

"No, I mean back in Washington."

"It's really my home," she said simply. "I love California, but this is really where I belong."

"In spite of all its hazards and pitfalls," he said with a sidelong glance. Jim Elrod uttered an encouraging if slightly nervous laugh from the back seat.

"I've made up my mind that I won't worry about them."

"I hope that's true," he said, "because they only exist in your own mind."

"So far," she said; and then added with a quick laugh that did not quite convince, "No, I don't mean that. I'll be a good girl."

"You do that," he said, only half-joking now, "because I'm going to be a good boy."

"You do *that,*" she said, "and I *really* won't worry."

But he knew, of course, that they were not at all sure of each other any more—an abandonment of customary habit so abrupt he still could not understand exactly how it had come about; unless it were indeed, as she had said, Washington, and some inherent power it seemed to have to change people.

Fortunately there was no time to linger on the ramifications of that: the driver of the limousine behind honked politely and he realized he had slowed to a virtual standstill while they spoke. He closed the gap obediently and then the whole line came to a halt as they rounded the curve in the drive and could see ahead. Tiny but commanding, Lyddie stood framed in her beautiful portico, aglow as always with fabulous jewels, over a pale mauve gown. Out of the limousine drawn up before her stepped two men and two women, the first of the women quite young, slim, attractive, the other, plumper, more homey. Lyddie greeted them with exclamations and kisses and waved them in, then turned to greet the husbands who followed. The first was tall, pleasant-faced, gray-haired, something in his manner identifying one who had been in politics a long time.

"Ham Delbacher!" she exclaimed, "you old Vice-President, you! Whoever would have thought it!"

"Certainly not I," Governor Delbacher said with a smile, bending down to kiss her powdery old cheek. "Lyddie, dear, how are you? You look marvelous, as always."

"I am, I am! I couldn't be better."

"And so nice of you to have us."

"I just wanted to be sure," she replied lightly, "that this administration gets started *right.*"

"And no better way to do it than with a party at Lyddie's," the second man, younger, taller, more handsome and somehow more determined-looking, remarked as he came forward to kiss her in his turn. "Lyddie darling, we shall be in your debt forever."

"I doubt that, Mr. President," she said with a chuckle, "but if I can keep you obligated for another ten minutes I'll be happy. Who knows what I might not be able to secure for myself in that time!"

"Everything your heart desires, Lyddie. Everything."

"Come," she said briskly, taking his arm and waving to the oncoming cars as the limousine pulled slowly away, "let's go in. It's going to start snowing again any minute."

And she bustled in, shooing them before her. Behind them four Secret Service men got out of the following car, puffing and blowing and slapping themselves to keep warm as they joined the police stationed unobtrusively in the shrubbery around the house.

Then the line moved forward. Mark and Linda and Jim Elrod in due course got out, followed immediately by Art Hampton and Chauncey Baron, in Art's aging Buick. The other guests came quickly, Janet Hardesty, Clem and Claretta Chisholm, Kal and Mele Tokumatsu, Rick Duclos, Senator and Mrs. Madison: forty in all. The great doors closed, they were sheltered in a warm, humming hive of glamorous and powerful people while Lyddie's maid and butler—one of the many pairs who hired out from night to night in Washington, familiar black faces that popped up at almost every party, old friends with whom warm greetings and news of families were exchanged—went efficiently about the gold-draped living room serving drinks and canapés.

Presently an informal receiving line formed spontaneously around the President-elect and his lady. Greetings were jovial, friendly, routine, until Senator Elrod, Mark and Linda approached. Then the President-elect's face lighted with an extra cordiality.

"Senator," he said, taking Jim Elrod's hand in both of his and presenting him to the new First Lady, "I'm delighted to see you. I look forward to a very pleasant association with you and the Armed Services Committee."

"I'm sure it will be, Mr. President," Jim Elrod said in his courtly way, "providin' we can just agree on a few little things."

"A few little ten-billion-dollar things?" the President-elect asked lightly. "Well, we'll have to see."

"Yes, sir," Jim Elrod agreed pleasantly, "that we will. You've met my daughter, Linda Rand Coffin, I believe? And my son-in-law, Senator Mark Coffin of California?"

"I haven't met your daughter," the President-elect said, "but I know it's going to be a great pleasure. Darling, this is Mrs. Coffin—and I don't *really* know your son-in-law, though we talked a couple of times during the campaign, didn't we, Mark?"

"Yes, sir," Mark said evenly. "And on the telephone, yesterday afternoon."

"Did we?" the President-elect asked comfortably.

"I'm talking to so many people these days I can hardly remember from minute to minute who I *have* talked to. Or, really, what most of them have to say."

"I thought it was a rather important conversation, myself," Mark said, trying to keep it light but finding it difficult to conceal his dismay. "At least to me, anyway. I'm sorry it didn't make any impression. I hoped it would, but I guess—being 'the Senate baby,' that awful tag I keep getting from the media all the time—it didn't register with you, did it, Mr. President?"

"Well, as I said," the President-elect replied easily, "I'm making about two hundred calls a day, I imagine. Everybody wants something—or"—he smiled disarmingly—"*I* want something—so it's hard to keep track."

"It may come up again," Mark said with a slightly edged pleasantness.

"No doubt," the President agreed, ignoring his tone. "Everything does, in politics. Art—!" And he greeted Senator Hampton with an easy, dismissing air.

"He knows perfectly well what we talked about," Mark said as they turned away. "Charlie Macklin for Attorney General. He even said he wanted to talk to me privately here tonight about it. What kind of a game is he trying to play, anyway?"

"Not so loud," Linda whispered hurriedly as she caught sight of Senator Madison nearby, straining to hear. "People will hear you."

"I don't much care if they do," Mark said grimly. "He and I are going to have to have an understanding."

"I'm sure he wants to have one," Senator Elrod said comfortably. "Why don't you just wait and see what happens? One of the secrets of Washington, at least so I've found, is—Wait—don't push too hard—let things unfold. They will. He can't acknowledge openly that you and he have been arguing about something. He hopes it can be worked out quietly between the two of you. That's by far the better way."

"Not on a matter of principle," Mark said, still grimly. Jim Elrod sighed in a half-humorous way.

"I suppose that applies to my bill, too."

"Yes, sir, that applies to your bill."

"There, too," Senator Elrod said gravely, "I think it had best be talked out privately first."

"I don't like this Washington passion for privacy in the public business!" Mark said, sounding really angry. His father-in-law looked equally annoyed, his wife apprehensive. The moment was saved by Jan Hardesty, who came over and gave Jim Elrod's arm an affectionate squeeze, something in it suggesting, for just a second, a deeper intimacy, soothing and instantly suppressed.

"Jim," she said lightly, "this looks like a family argument, and Lyddie's is no place for that. Tell me, are we going to get your bill through?"

"That's part of the argument," Senator Elrod said, relaxing under the persuasion of her charm. "Our young firebrand here thinks he may be against it."

"I'm not *sure* I will be," Mark protested, somewhat desperately. "I don't *know* at the moment. I just want to be *convinced,* that's all. Doesn't anybody think I have a right to have the arguments presented to me? Am I supposed to take everything on faith? What do you think, Senator? You've been here for a while."

"Too long, I sometimes think," Senator Hardesty said with a smile. "And it's 'Jan,' of course, as I told you earlier today, not 'Senator.' Yes, I think you have a right to have the arguments presented to you.

I'm with Jim on this one, though, as I usually am on defense matters. We're dropping dangerously far behind."

"I still think we have an ample atomic arsenal, ample throw-weight, ample force, to meet any threat," Mark said stubbornly. "I'm not saying yet that I can't be convinced—"

"But you doubt it," Jan said, still lightly. "Well, we'll surely try, won't we, Jim? What's your argument with the President, Mark?"

"Do I have one?" Mark asked, suddenly bland, deciding he could play the game like everyone else.

"A slight difference of opinion, we all gathered."

"Oh no," he said. "Actually, *I've* forgotten what we talked about on the telephone, too."

"Sure, sure," she said, taking his arm. "I think Lyddie's about to go into her it's-time-to-eat routine. I think she wants us to drift into the dining room, and I believe you're my partner. So let's drift."

And with animated chatter about this and that and nothing much, she eased him along into the ornate dining room, its long table covered with gold damask cloth and napkins, gold candlesticks, gleaming vermeil flatware, three wineglasses at every place, the full ambience of a formal Washington dinner.

Not by accident, Lyddie had placed the President-elect on her right, Mark on her left; and when everyone was seated, she clasped her hands together and with a satisfied smile said, "Now! Mr. President, would you say grace?"

And after thinking for a moment, he did so in a grave and measured voice:

"Lord, bless this food and we who are about to eat it. Bless dear Lyddie for gathering us together so that we may partake of her gracious hospitality and get to know one another better.

"Bless this nation and all of us who seek to serve her; give us strength to do our best for her, in whatever office we may bold.

"Help this country, which is of good purpose and good heart, however imperfect she may be, and help her people, who were born to great ideals and believe in them still, however hard the still unfinished path to their accomplishment may be.

"Preserve and protect this nation and its people in these difficult days. Lead them safely through: for though their ways be not perfect, their hearts and purposes are good. Keep them safe and let them continue to live as free people: for they have much yet to do in Your world.

"Amen."

For a moment they all sat solemn and touched; then animated conversation resumed all down the table as soup was served.

"Well!" Lyddie said, clasping her hands again in her characteristically youthful gesture. "Isn't this nice!"

"It's delightful," the President-elect said. "As always in your house, dear Lyddie. Mark, you must cultivate this lady. She's the key to all power in Washington."

"He doesn't have to cultivate me," Lyddie said, while conversation down the table quieted as many tried to listen without appearing to do so. "I love him already! He's always going to be welcome in this house—where I hope, as tonight, he will always meet friends." And she gave the President-elect a bright and birdlike beam. He smiled.

"I'm sure that will always be the case, Lyddie. I'm sure he will make friends wherever he goes. He has millions already, as witness California. Thank God he does have them! Otherwise *I* wouldn't be here!"

And he gave Mark a frank and charmingly disarming smile that brought applause and laughter from down the table.

"Then why—" Mark began with a muffled but obvious exasperation. But Jan Hardesty's quick hand on his arm stopped that at once.

"Senator," she said crisply, deliberately reminding him of who he now was, "when the President-elect of the United States says he owes his victory to you, don't argue. Just tuck it away for future reference. It's something we all wish we had."

Again there was laughter, in which the President comfortably joined, though his eyes were not quite so amused when they met Mark's. Down the table Rick Duclos leaned across Claretta Chisholm to murmur to Kal Tokumatsu, "What's eating our boy, with the President?"

"I don't know," Kal murmured back, "but I think I'll talk to him about letting it show in public."

"It's no way to make points at the White House," Claretta agreed. "Particularly when he should be in such good shape with the man—as he admits Mark is."

Across the table Linda, nervously aware of their quiet exchange though she could not quite hear it, turned to Chauncey Baron on her right and said briskly,

"So, Mr. Secretary, we're going to have you back in Foggy Bottom for another tour of duty."

"That's right," he said, looking down upon her from his towering height in a fatherly way. "Do you think Mark would like to be on the Foreign Relations Committee?"

"He'd be absolutely thrilled to death," Linda said,

pleased expression indicating that she would be, too. "Do you think there's the remotest chance, for a freshman?"

"There might be," Chauncey said; and added in a lower tone, "Providing he doesn't antagonize anybody."

"Yes," she said, expression suddenly worried. "I know. He *is* upset with the President about something, but he musn't let it affect his whole career right at the beginning. He's also upset with Daddy's bill, and he doesn't realize that Daddy can be a pretty tough opponent, too. He just knows him as a kindly old father-in-law, not as one of the shrewdest operators in the Senate."

"He has a lot to learn," Chauncey observed. "But" —in a kindly tone—"he's a very smart boy. He will."

"I hope so," Linda said, rather bleakly.

"There, there," Chauncey said, touched by her concern. "Don't worry. He will."

But elsewhere along the table, they were not so sure. Art Hampton and Jim Elrod, seated next to one another at this party at which widowed and older public men predominated, were concerned.

"Oh, he's got all the potential in the world," Senator Hampton agreed. "There's nowhere he can't go in this town if he'll just not be too impatient—and if he'll learn that there are times when principle has to bend just a little if it's not to be broken by superior power."

"He seems to think the White House isn't superior power," Jim Elrod said with a rueful humor. "He also seems to have the same opinion about me."

"What, on your bill?"

"Yes, he sounds as though he'd like to lead the parade against it, which I don't think would be wise—at least, I'd rather he didn't."